# The Cuffer Anthology

## A Selection of Short Fiction

© 2009, Pam Frampton

We gratefully acknowledge the financial support of the Canada Council for the Arts, the Government of Canada through the Book Publishing Industry Development Program (BPIDP), and the Government of Newfoundland and Labrador through the Department of Tourism, Culture and Recreation for our publishing program.

All rights reserved. No part of this work covered by the copyrights hereon may be reproduced or used in any form or by any means—graphic, electronic or mechanical—without the prior written permission of the publisher. Any requests for photocopying, recording, taping or information storage and retrieval systems of any part of this book shall be directed in writing to the Canadian Reprography Collective, One Yonge Street, Suite 1900, Toronto, Ontario M5E 1E5.

Cover design and layout by Todd Manning
Printed on acid-free paper

Published by
KILLICK PRESS
an imprint of CREATIVE BOOK PUBLISHING
a Transcontinental Inc. associated company
P.O. Box 8660, Stn. A
St. John's, Newfoundland and Labrador A1B 3T7

Printed in Canada by:
TRANSCONTINENTAL INC.

Library and Archives Canada Cataloguing in Publication

The Cuffer anthology : a selection of short fiction / edited by Pam Frampton.

ISBN 978-1-897174-46-3

1. Short stories, Canadian (English)--Newfoundland and Labrador.
2. Canadian fiction (English)--21st century. I. Frampton, Pam

PS8329.5.N3C83 2009      C813'.01089718      C2009-903862-5

# The Cuffer Anthology
## A Selection of Short Fiction

Edited by Pam Frampton

St. John's, Newfoundland and Labrador
2009

# Introduction

Back in early 2008, when we were mulling over the idea of a creating a literary prize at The Telegram, we decided practically from the start that we wanted to celebrate and encourage the writing of short fiction.

There were two reasons for that.

First, because shorter pieces of writing are what we specialize in at The Telegram — though granted, we work in fact, not fiction (and trust me, the truth really can be the stranger of the two).

And second, because we felt that with short stories we would be able to publish some of the best entries in the newspaper, as well as consider compiling an anthology in partnership with Creative Book Publishing, and in that way expose as much local talent as we could.

The name Cuffer, by the way, was chosen because it refers to a short tale, or yarn. Well, we received tales of all descriptions when submissions came flooding in for the inaugural Cuffer Prize.

Unlike generations ago, when the works of local authors were rarely taught in school, and seeing a book from Newfoundland and Labrador on a library shelf was the exception, not the rule, today this province can lay claim to an abundance of world-class writers.

Now, books by authors like Michael Crummey, Lisa Moore and Bernice Morgan can be found cheek by jowl with books from Margaret Atwood, Salman Rushdie and Gabriel Garcia Marquez.

There seems to be a new confidence in the writing we're producing; a stronger sense of who and where we are, and of our place in the world, that is encouraging to anyone who loves to read literature grounded and steeped in this place we call home.

And really, why couldn't a story set in Rushoon be every bit as interesting as one that unfolds in Rome? Why not Pasadena, N.L., instead of Pasadena, Calif.? Who needs New York when you've got New World Island?

That confidence was evident in many of the submissions we received for the Cuffer Prize.

Stories like our three winning entries — Josh Pennell's "The Last Haiku," Gail Alice Collins' "The Black and White Cat," and Chad Pelley's "Subtle Differences," are universal in their themes of love, loneliness and sacrifice, but they are uniquely local, with rich detail: a dark pub on the St. John's harbour front; a saltbox house out around the bay where an elderly couple scatters birdseed in the driveway; a law office on Duckworth Street where a quiet, dignified man is treated shabbily by his coworkers.

There are many other themes, too, that will resonate with Newfoundland and Labrador readers everywhere: the rural and urban divide; the feared loss of a way of life; change and resettlement; death and acceptance; betrayal and alienation; a love/hate relationship with the sea.

And storytelling. Always, great storytelling.

From the gooseflesh horror of Jaime Pynn George's "Uncle Ned's Turnips" to the clever tricksterism of Robert C. Parsons' "The Flower of Irishville," there are some great yarns here waiting to be discovered.

We hope you enjoy them as much as we did, and that you will eagerly anticipate hearing more from these talented authors in the future.

If you've purchased this book, thank you for supporting writers who are telling this province's story to the world, and for contributing to a project whose proceeds will be used to boost literacy in Newfoundland and Labrador.

Enjoy this collection, and tell your friends about it.

If you submitted a story to the Cuffer Prize, thanks for sharing your time and talents with us. It was a pleasure to peek into the imaginations of writers from across the province.

Thanks, especially, to all those whose works are collected here. You are not only in great company, but you have pooled your talents to help nurture and inspire readers and writers of the future.

**Pam Frampton**
**St. John's**

# Cuffer Prize Anthology 2008

## stories

**The Last Haiku,** by Josh Pennell ..................... 1
**The Black and White Cat,** by Gail Alice Collins ........ 7
**Subtle Differences,** by Chad Pelley .................. 15
**Macaroni and Cheese,** by Susan Chalker Browne ...... 21
**From the Pen of Pym,** by Adam Clarke ............... 27
**Unsettled,** by Annette Conway ...................... 31
**Adventure on Signal Hill,** by Michael Nolan ......... 37
**Snares,** by Michael Nolan .......................... 43
**Blue Fish,** by J.L. Scurlock ......................... 47
**Requiem for Monica,** by Deborah Whelan ........... 53
**The Stick Shift,** by Owen Whelan ................... 59
**Friday Night,** by Richard Barnes .................... 65
**The Manor,** by Gerard Collins ...................... 71
**Under the Flake,** by Jim Combden .................. 77
**The Purse,** by Mark Hoffe .......................... 83
**Hunted,** by Heather Lane .......................... 89
**The Rock,** by Ruby Mann ........................... 95
**The Flower of Irishville,** by Robert C. Parsons ........ 99
**How Far is Nowhere?,** by Chad Pelley ............... 103
**The Dixie Challenger,** by Benedict Pittman .......... 107
**The Inheritance,** by Martin Poole ................... 113
**The Passing,** by Marilyn Pumphrey ................. 119
**Uncle Ned's Turnips,** by Jaime Pynn George ......... 125
**The Boom Run,** by Peter Daniel Shea ............... 129
**Buried Treasure,** by Tina Mardel Stewart ............ 133

# The Last Haiku

## by Josh Pennell

*Winner of The Cuffer Prize 2008*

He wrote the world into Haikus. The poems were neither brilliant nor forgettable. His first came when he was quite young, certainly no older than 10.

His father was rarely around, which affected him very little.

His mother claimed to love to be alone, but on Friday nights while he was out playing spotlight, she would do her hair up in an '80s hurricane, slip into one of her dresses and sit alone among the lines of candles that flickered before her like worshipping monks.

Slipping away from the game, he would sit, gargoyle-like, in one of the maples that gated his front yard and watch his mother sip wine in the candlelight, while her favourite records spun their songs and then scratched the needle's longing.

One night while she rubbed the lipstick from the rim of her finest wineglass and held her face in her hands, he took a small pocket-knife he had found along the riverbank.

Hunched in the tree, he chipped away at the bark between his knees.

A *lipstick bruised wineglass*
A *boy sees unseen*
A *woman sits alone*

That was the first, but more would follow. He would write 10 a night or go two years without lifting a pen.

Watching a torpored fly buzz to life on the windowsill one February day, he wrote:

In *a beam of winter light*
A *fly awakens*
To *an early death*

On a path in Butterpot Park one December when he was 17, he came across the tracks of an adult and child.

He followed them through the crowded spruce until he found a gathering of snowmen in a clearing, all facing each other, heads bowed either in greeting or with the burden of Avalon winds. In his book that night he wrote

*A child's prints in winter*
*Lead the way to where*
*Only small things matter*

During a period working for Hydro on the threaded highways and railways of Northern Ontario that rumbled with lumber trucks bursting with wood and trains empty of people, he sat waiting for a left-turn signal. He looked down at his fingers curled around the steering wheel and saw that his hands were just like his father's: thick, cracked and capable. He pulled over and cried, not for any sense of longing but for the passage of time that was pushing him along much too fast and into a way of life he neither wanted nor understood. He was 25 when he wrote:

*I turn the car left*
*And look down into the wheel*
*At my father's hands*

He was 26 before he started living. It was then that he laid to rest some of the images from his past. The people who recognized him after his time in Northern Ontario said there was something lighter about him, as though he had sweat out whatever macabre feelings he harboured while working the saw in the thick Ontario heat.

One night after a stroll along the St. John's harbour front, where the stern lines of foreign boats bent the winds into strange tunes, he walked into a dark pub. There he recognized a young Australian woman who had taught him an English course during his short attempt at university. She had finished her master's quite young and was not so much older than him when she was hired to fill in for a professor for a single term.

Their conversation came easy. They spoke mostly about their favourite writers and also the strangeness of time, how it seemed to stretch on forever and yet be lost like loose change. He wrote in his book while she was in the washroom and let her catch him on her return. He left the book open on the table while he went for drinks and smiled over his shoulder as she tried to read his words without moving closer.

She asked him to walk her home. She walked through her door silently and continued up the stairs. He watched her from behind until he heard her bedroom door open from somewhere deep inside the old house, groaning like the call of a trenched whale.

He followed and found her undressing in front of a mirrored nightstand, her hair untied and running the crucifix of freckles along her back and shoulders.

Afterwards, she lay on his chest and spoke about Australia. He liked the sound of that island. Down Under. Down under all of this. Down to the bottom of everything. He fell asleep listening to her. When he awoke, the sun was on her face.

They loved each other very much. They would walk together with their arms around each other's waist, whispering whatever secrets they hadn't already told. It was as though one tried to outdo the other for how much of themselves they could share.

He let it all out. Every fear and dream, every time he felt guilty about being happy.

It frightened her how much she loved him. She would tell him how overwhelmed and scared she felt and he would smile, not understanding the ways of a woman and thinking that could only be a good thing.

At some point, the greatness of it all faded for her. It seemed to her he was clinging onto the feelings of the first time they met. He wrote Haikus about her as though he was looking at her for the first time, but instead of this making her feel as though the magic of it all would never wear off, it made her feel as though he wasn't capable of growing. He wouldn't let go of the first time he truly felt happy so he could find new occasions to smile.

She left him.

For a time he didn't seem to care. His life became one of routines. Rise, walk, write, eat, sleep. Gradually he walked longer, slept less and ate nothing. One day he just kept on going. He walked to the other side of The Narrows and up the old riverbed near Fort Amherst. He huddled somewhere along the top as night fell. The storm petrels rose as darkness fell, weaving in and out of the fog that glowed dull in the smothered moonlight. Their ghoulish laughter taunted him. He listened for a time and lashed out once, swinging his arms wildly, hoping to smash them out of the sky. They weaved their way through the night-time, filling the blackness with their strange sound.

By morning he was almost gone. He clung to the small notebook he always kept with him, his other hand crushing a cheap pen. The petrels were gone.

Back out at sea and down underground. The skies shone bright with July sun. Below him pods of whales rolled in deep water. Gannets fell around them from the sky, exploding on the ocean's surface only to rise intact, as though the ocean had repaired them.

He watched them in their strange dance, the whales twisting in the shower of seabirds. Everything inviting him. All creatures pointing the way. He took out his book and wrote his last Haiku.

*Blue rests upon blue*
*Voices invite me in*
*To the land down under.*

JOSH PENNELL describes himself as "a pessimistic wannabe conservationist turned mediocre journalist." He lives in St. John's, where his career goal is to be debt-free.

# The Black and White Cat

## by Gail Alice Collins

*2nd-place winner of The Cuffer Prize 2008*

It was June, when the little black and white cat first appeared on the bridge of the white saltbox house. It sat next to the barbecue, which was still tarped down after a long winter. The little cat sniffed the tarp: it was sure cats had been here before.

Inside the kitchen, the curtain flickered.

"Nellie, come here," the white-haired man said.

"What is it?" asked the white-haired woman.

"A cat," said the man, in wonderment.

"Drive it out of it," said the white-haired woman.

She rapped on the window. The cat sprang off the bridge.

"No more cats," said the woman. "It's too hard when they go."

All day the white-haired man rocked in his chair by the window, watching the garden.

Early the next morning, the cat crept across the driveway – which was littered with birdseed – to eat the cat treats that had materialized on the bridge overnight.

"That cat is driving away the birds," said the woman.

"She's a nice little cat," said the man.

When his daughter called from St. John's, the man waited patiently for his turn to talk on the phone. He told his daughter all about the little black and white cat.

"Why don't you keep her?" asked his daughter.

"Your mother, your mother ..." he said.

"She loves cats, too," said the daughter.

"Yes, but ..." said the father.

"I know," said the daughter

"When are you coming home again?" asked the father.

"Soon," said the daughter, vaguely.

The white-haired man watched through the window. In the garden, the white-haired woman crouched beside a cardboard box. In her hand was a string attached to a flap at the top of the box. Inside the box, there was a tiny pile of cat treats.

The cat sat behind the woman, observing her strange behaviour.

In July, the daughter came home for a visit.

"What happened to the black and white cat?" she asked.

"We took her to the cabin," said her father.

They drove the five kilometres to their cabin, in another cove of the same bay.

The couple showed their daughter the shirt-lined box under the cabin and the bowl that was filled with warm milk every day.

"Every day?" asked the daughter.

"Every day," said her father.

"Look," said the white-haired woman, "there's another shrew in her food bowl. The cat is trying to earn her keep."

"What's her name?" asked the daughter.

"Kitty," said her mother.

"Kitty?" said the daughter.

"We don't want to get too attached," said her mother.

In her apartment on Springdale Street, the daughter phoned her parents around the bay. There was no answer. The next day she called again.

"I was worried," she said.

"We slept at the cabin to keep Kitty company," said her father.

"Why don't you just bring her home?" asked the daughter.

"Perhaps," said the mother.

In August, the daughter dropped by the outport on her way to meet friends in Salvage.

Kitty was sitting on a cat perch in the window, watching the birds flutter around the driveway.

Her mother showed her the quilt she'd made for the cat.

"Just old scraps of material," she said.

"She sleeps with us," said the father. "She's jumpy at night. I have to come downstairs with her if she wants a drink of water."

The daughter scratched Kitty behind the ear. Kitty tilted her head obligingly and began to purr.

In September, the white-haired couple came to Springdale Street. The father had an appointment with a specialist at the Health Sciences.

Kitty had to be coaxed out from under the bed in the spare room.

"She didn't like the ride," the white-haired woman said. "She doesn't like cars."

The daughter was working long hours at the Confederation Building.

Her parents ventured to the mall on their own and came back proudly bearing a new toaster and some tea towels for her apartment.

At the end of the week, the daughter got a call at work.

"I thought you were leaving this morning," said the daughter.

"Kitty's gone," said her father. "When I opened the car door, she jumped out."

"It was his fault," said the mother.

"I thought she was holding on to her," said the father.

The three of them searched up and down the steep hill that is Springdale Street. They spoke to boys playing in the shortcuts across to Casey Street. They looked under a bridge on Coronation Street.

Her parents went home without the cat, bereft.

The daughter called the SPCA. She put an ad in the paper and an announcement on the radio.

The daughter started to get calls replying to her ad.

She went to the rectory of a neighbourhood church. The stray was a tabby.

She was called to a home on Patrick Street. The cat was coal black.

A man called, saying he'd tell her more about the cat when she came to his apartment.

An older woman called to say she hadn't found a cat, she just wanted to say how sorry she felt.

The daughter walked up and down the hills of the west end, searching.

At the Confederation Building, her co-workers commented on her weight loss. "You look great," they said.

She went home and weighed herself. She'd lost eight pounds looking for Kitty.

Every night at 10, her parents called.

"No news," she said.

Over a latte at the Java Jive, she asked a friend, "Could this somehow be my fault?"

"You weren't even there, " said the friend.

Her mother told her her father was depressed.

"He won't eat properly. I told him we shouldn't get a cat. Why did you encourage him?"

The daughter saw a black and white cat outside a new brownstone.

She crouched down for a closer look. She couldn't quite remember. Did Kitty have a white spot just there? An expensive-looking woman came down the steps.

"Annabelle," she said, "Annabelle," lifting the cat into her arms.

Her mother called, saying her father was grieving.

The daughter suggested getting another cat. The mother slammed down the receiver.

The white-haired couple came back to St. John's. The father had another appointment. He looked smaller, depleted somehow. The mother was out of sorts after the long car ride.

The daughter felt some trepidation.

"I have something to tell you," she said. "I may have found Kitty."

Her father looked shocked.

"May?" asked her mother.

"Come see," said the daughter.

She opened the door to the spare bedroom. There were three black and white cats on the windowsill. Ten black and white cats lay curled up on the bed.

A black tail trailed out from under the bedskirt. The room was filled with black and white cats.

"Kitty," said the father. And all the little black and white cats came running.

GAIL ALICE COLLINS is originally from Dover, Bonavista Bay. Her scripts have been produced for radio and television. She now works for CBC Radio in Gander.

# Subtle Differences

## by Chad Pelley

*3rd-place winner of The Cuffer Prize 2008*

Every day, Mom would hand Dad a cup of coffee as he stormed through the kitchen towards the garage door. He'd grab it from her – stuffing three thick fingers, not four, into the handle – take one huge gulp and, still moving, crash the black mug down onto the countertop. Then the coffee would splash up out of the cup and slap down onto the counter.

There were always rings of coffee on the countertop. Sticky, perfect circles. Sometimes they'd criss-cross to make eights, or infinity symbols. Mickey Mouse, a snowman. On the weeks Mom was too tired to clean the kitchen, they'd link up to make the Olympic rings. Maybe I spent more time looking into those rings, like a Rorschach test, than I did with my father.

And then he'd come home – always just as Mom was putting the supper on the table – all rundown looking. As if he'd just fought Mike Tyson and lost, or spent the day running from a pack of wolves. When he sat at the table to eat, he fell into that seat like it was a wheelchair. Like his legs gave out at 5:15 every weeknight.

His legs worked just fine by six though. He'd slip outside, quietly, tiptoeing almost, as if the whole world was an egg about to crack and he didn't want to be covered in yolk.

He'd slide into that picnic table, cup of black coffee in one hand, a book the size of the Bible in another, and binoculars around his neck. It was understood we were not to follow him.

At least he smiled and talked a bit more when he came back in. He'd at least ask for some dessert or help me with my Science and Math homework, because they weren't Mom's thing. English was.

But most days Dad was just the guy who slammed his coffee down in the mornings, ate supper in silence, and stared into the forest behind our house for hours on end – as if it were a wishing well and he was rich.

And then Grade 3 came along, and Career Week. On the first Thursday in April, Dad had to take me to work with him.

"Brace yourself, kiddo."

I asked him where we'd be going and he said one of the lawyers' offices down on Duckworth Street.

One of them, he'd said. As if they were all the same to him.

I remember an elevator ding when we hit the fourth floor. I remember that door opening and hearing a man yelling into a phone using more curse words than nouns. Most adults stop swearing when they realize they are in the presence of a kid. Not him. I found it weird he didn't even wave to my father. On TV, everyone in a place of work was friends; the lack of solidarity here caught me offguard.

It meant the day wasn't going to be any fun.

I followed Dad through a maze of grey-carpeted cubicles, and when he stopped walking, I banged face-first into his behind: "Go ahead, step into my cage, Son."

He opened the door to his office. His was smaller than the rest, I guess because he wasn't actually a lawyer. I never did figure what he was, and at the time, it seemed right not to ask him to explain. But now I know what God would feel like if we all had access to Him: totally rundown. People found every way to yell and complain at the poor man. Mail, e-mail, over the phone, over-the-phone conference calls, in person. I think maybe there was one guy up in the ceiling vents yelling down at him: "Damn you, Porter, it's your fault, just ... because!"

It seemed like everything was his fault. It seemed like his job was to be the one to blame. One man, who looked strikingly similar to Johnny Cash, yelled at Dad because his secretary messed something up. The guy's words came out coated in saliva. Clear dots formed on his tie, and then one huge blob came out; like a stick with a ball on both ends, a dumbbell, and nailed Dad right in the eye. He didn't even flinch. He didn't even blink. You'd think he should've blinked. I guess he was so used to it, maybe, or he was that rundown and numbed by his job that he could take spit in his eye and not blink. I found that pretty sad.

One thing was clear: They took their 10:30 coffee break quite seriously. It was like some invisible alarm clock had gone off at 10:20. Without a word from anyone, a lineup had formed in front of Dad's desk and they littered his tabletop with coins and scraps of paper detailing their coffee and snack orders. One guy wrote in all capital letters, and used three exclamation marks – CREAM NOT MIK!!! – as if Dad was stupid, even though he was the one who had spelled milk without an L. Dad wrote all the orders out on the back of one of those pink slips of paper used for phone messages.

"Put on yer jacket, kiddo. This is the best part of the day. Auntie Crae's frozen yogurt. Ever had it?"

So they got coffee, and he got a frozen yogurt.

"Coffee leaches calcium from your bones, Jacob. Anyone ever tell you that before?"

He got me a bakeapple frozen yogurt, just like his. I pretended all those seeds grinding against my teeth never bothered me, even though it felt like biting into beetles. It tasted OK, but I probably would've ordered blueberry. The kind of ice cream Mom usually bought me.

I remember walking up that semi-winding staircase that connects George Street and Duckworth. I asked him what made him want to be a "... whatever you are."

He was chewing the gritty frozen yogurt like bubble gum when he answered me. Every few steps he'd lay the tray of coffee down on top of something so he could take a scoop.

"That's not how it works for most people, kiddo. I'd have liked to have been a conservation biologist, the next Suzuki maybe. But one thing leads to another, and there are bills to be paid, and, well, someone's gotta raise you, right?"

He messed up my hair with his hands and smiled.

"We should finish these treats and toss out the containers before we head back in."

There was another stained-orange ice cream cup in that can, and I wondered if it was his from yesterday.

That night, after supper, I stood in the doorway, watching Dad watching the trees. He must've saw me there. He turned around, put a finger perpendicular to his lips to silence me, but flapped his other hand urgently as if to say, C'mere, but quickly, quietly.

I mimicked his eggshell walk. He handed me the binoculars, and waited until I'd seen the bird to fill me in, in case his voice scared it away.

White-winged crossbill!

He snatched his binoculars back and handed me a book on birds opened to page 312. Family Fringillidae: The Finches and relatives. There was a picture of a white-winged crossbill, with lines pointing to all of its distinguishing features. Bright red body. Black wings and tail. Two bold and white wing bars. But still, the thing looked an awful lot like the bird on the next page, the red crossbill.

I closed the book, but he looked at me, and I didn't want to seem uninterested. I wasn't. So I pretended I was just checking out the front cover. It was glossy, and full of pictures of birds with his thumbprints all over them. I looked at the spine; the book was thick and had maybe 9,000 birds in it. That was a lot of reasons to sit and wait every night like Dad did. He scanned the trees with his binoculars like a sniper. He'd shift to the left when he heard a rustle in the trees, or glance up when he heard a whistle.

I let the book unfold in my laps. Family Laridae: The Gulls. I had no idea there were so many.

I thought a seagull was a seagull. Now I know the difference between the ring-billed gull, and the herring gull, and the black-backed gull, and the Icelandic gull.

Now I know life's not that simple.

CHAD PELLEY is an emerging writer from St. John's and a member of the Writer's Alliance of Newfoundland and Labrador. In January 2008, his manuscript won him competitive entry into WANL's mentorship program, and he writes a regular book column for Current magazine.

# Macaroni and Cheese

## by Susan Chalker Browne

*Cuffer Prize 2008 Honourable Mention*

Nineteen days after my mother's death, someone rings my front doorbell. I pad listlessly down the hall, as the desolate grey of a March afternoon in St. John's sucks colour from the silk flowers on the table and blurs the framed photos on the wall. Strange to hear the front doorbell. No one uses that door when the snow is on the ground. We don't shovel it out.

"I always say the best time to bring food is three weeks later," says Kate Hanlon, her words tumbling out in a torrent. "There's so much ham and turkey in the beginning and nowhere to store any of it. But after a while that's all gone and maybe you're having a sad day, and maybe that's the best time to bring something for dinner."

I smile at the sight of her. I have known this woman all my life, although we have never been close. Dressed in a down-filled burgundy jacket, her mousy hair tosses like hay in the wind, her face plain and kind and devoid of any makeup. I invite her in from the cold, apologizing for the pine needles littering the concrete steps. "Leftover from the Christmas tree," I say ruefully, forcefully shutting the door against the March gale.

"It's my mother's recipe," continues Kate, in a manner of brisk authority. "Her signature is the breadcrumb topping which my kids always fight over. Heat it on 350 for thirty minutes. There's plenty here for all your crowd."

I take the tinfoil casserole from her and it feels heavy and warm in the palms of my hands. Shifting it to one side, I hug Kate awkwardly, tears burning inside my eyelids. This is a woman I never expected to see at my door with macaroni and cheese. In the last few years her marriage has crumbled away and she has stared down breast cancer. I watch her lumber back down my steps and pick her way over a bare patch of brown grass that has broken through the snow.

"How's the mac 'n' cheese?" I ask my teenage offspring as they hulk around the kitchen table that evening. The warmth from the oven has overheated the small room, cocooning us against the black and icy night.

"Good," they mumble, mouths full of food.

"Except for the topping," adds Steven. "That tastes weird."

On the Saturday that Mom is admitted to Palliative Care, my cousin Libby brings macaroni and cheese to my house. The day starts off normally enough – the familiar gnawing dread in my stomach as I unload the dishwasher and drive my daughter to basketball. Mom had fallen the previous day. Slipped on snow, my father said, coming out of The Cellar restaurant. (And I worried, had she slipped or collapsed?) Dad and I had pleaded with her not to go out for lunch.

"Too many people are telling me what to do!" she had retorted, in that dignified, imperious tone. And so we said nothing else.

Driving down in the ambulance, my mother lies prone on the stretcher like she's already dead. The white fur of her jacket hood circles her face, clear tubing for the oxygen trails from her nose. My cellphone rings.

"Libby's bringing mac 'n' cheese for dinner," says my husband.

"How sweet," I say. "We're on our way to the Miller Centre now." My voice sounds calm and controlled, like it's coming from another person.

There are no real windows in the back of an ambulance. Did you know that? I peer around to the front, where the two paramedics make lazy comments to each other like it's any other day. White picket fences appear suddenly in the windshield, and the corner of a green clapboard house, and the moving red mirage of a minivan. A sign saying 'Wyatt Park' flashes by, and then I know where we are.

"Libby's bringing macaroni and cheese for dinner," I say to Mom, as I fold the cellphone back into my purse.

She smiles weakly. "Good," she says, as her eyelids flutter shut again.

Later that night, at home, my feet are sweaty and swollen from wearing heavy boots all day. I had hurriedly pulled them on, to run Amy down to practice, then to quickly check in on Mom and Dad. Thick winter boots, clomping through the corridors of Palliative Care. Here is the chapel, a phone in the family room that anyone can use, and these chairs fold out into beds if you want to stay the night.

Libby's macaroni and cheese sits loosely covered on the kitchen counter. Half-eaten, cold, congealed. "Is it good?" I ask, lumping some onto a plate to warm in the microwave.

"Not bad," says my husband, pouring me a glass of white wine. "A bit dry. Different than yours."

Tromping up the side of Signal Hill, from Queen's Battery to Cabot Tower, the April sun is crystal clean and cold. Wind cuts into your face, shoots sharply into your lungs, and cleanses. Below us, seagulls glide over the dark water that churns and beats against the solid rock walls of The Narrows. I feel intensely alive, and wonder, is that wrong?

Beside me, Aunt Jane is puffing but keeping pace. Amazing energy. I smile as I watch her. We share a quirky humour and foolish sense of fun that Mom never quite got into. I sometimes worried that she minded my close attachment to her sister. But on the day she was diagnosed with cancer, Mom asked her sister Jane to come with us to the doctor. "It will be easier for Susan if you're there, too."

She's talking about her grandchildren, my Aunt Jane, how she made them macaroni and cheese on a day when their mother was busy. "They love my macaroni," she says with satisfaction. "I layer it for them. First the noodles, then the butter, then the cheese." Her hand makes each layer in the air.

"No milk?" I ask, thinking of my own recipe.

"No milk," she says quickly, her chin firm and set. "Never milk. Only butter."

And I remember the night before, and my own macaroni and cheese. The shredded orange mounds of old cheddar piled upon my worn breadboard. The creamy white sauce tenderly whisked into thickness. The slippery noodles falling into the colander, steam rising and fogging my cold kitchen windows.

Then suddenly it occurs to me, about Mom's mac 'n' cheese. Strangely, I can't say for sure how it was. Was it creamy or somewhat dry, made with butter and no milk, or was it finished off with crusty breadcrumbs?

An ordinary question – and no way to find the answer. The enormity of it overwhelms me. My hand grips hard the weathered grey wood of the handrail and I stop upon the trail to catch my breath.

SUSAN CHALKER BROWNE is an award-winning writer, journalist and teacher. She has written several children's books, including "Freddy's Day at the Races" and "The Land of a Thousand Whales." She lives in St. John's with her husband and four children.

# From the Pen of Pym

## by Adam Clarke

*Cuffer Prize 2008 Honourable Mention*

Jan. 19
Attn: Mr. Robert Kilfoy and Associates

Hello, boys. I have become aware that Chairman Kilfoy and certain other members of the committee have voiced doubts about my research over the last two months. Some of you have probably considered freezing the funding for my experiments due to delays in its completion. That is why I'm addressing you all in this letter, as I believe that the results of the last few trial runs have been seen by some as a failure. Failure. Such a dreadful word when isolated from a sentence, is it not? If "failure" were a person, surely it would be a brutish Gestapo officer with a dental-drill fetish who moonlights as a phys ed teacher.

My apologies, I have digressed somewhat from the subject at hand. As you know, I have spent the last 18 months devising and testing the prototype of the Memory Intelligence Management System (or MIMS). Naturally, I am grateful for the untold millions of dollars invested into building the machine and, rather than aborting this costly research, I request to renew funding for the next year. The potential reward and profitability of it could set Estram-Axos Ltd. at the top of the corporate food chain. After all, MIMS (an acronym that my assistants have determined to be cute) will offer people the opportunity to access and edit the sections of the brain where memories are stored. Once the quirks are worked out, we stand to gain for its potential as a tool for the medical industry as well as the military-industrial complex. Do not let a sudden need for penny-pinching thwart this new discovery. Stop thinking as investors and imagine yourselves as frontiersmen employing me as a divining rod in your quest for water. Remember, the water in this case will sustain human beings in a way no liquid could ever hope to.

While the project has had a few stumbling blocks, are they so severe as to necessitate halting my work? Animal testing has been fruitful and our first and only human subject has been a great success. The test subject – a middle-aged security guard – came to us with the hopes of erasing his every negative memory. With only two treatments, or "MIMprints," as we call them, the subject had shown no awareness of any suffering, disappointment or embarrassment at any point in his life.

Yes, the subject went directly to the home of his former spouse after final MIMprintation, allegedly breaking in when his keys failed to open the front door. Yes, he had to be restrained and forcibly removed by police. Yes, he proceeded to name me, my assistants and this company by name when interrogated the following morning. Omelettes and broken eggs, gentlemen. If we refrain from allowing science to shake up a few divorce proceedings, we aren't just hurting ourselves. We're hurting the human heart. With as little as $15 million, I can, in all likelihood, have this ready before Halloween.

Let's make this happen.

Sincerely,
Dr. Gerald Pym

\* \* \* \*

Aug. 31
Attn: Mr. Robert Kilfoy and Associates

When I was called up to the boardroom this morning, I had assumed that my written request earlier this week had fully convinced you of the importance of this project. Instead, the tongue-lashing both my project and I received crossed the lines of constructive criticism. The pain your words have caused me, gentlemen, goes well and beyond any venomous epithet ever thrown in my direction. Not even during my tenure as a rescuer of distempered parrots have I endured such hateful verbiage. Frankly, I would've expected the newly formed Newfoundland Science Council to be a little more chummy with me ...

Rather than defeating me, however, I see your dismissal as a challenge. Even without funding or my assistants, I can still operate the MIMS. I will show you just how successful it can be by testing it on none other than myself. I shall wipe all memory of your monstrous slurs this morning and, as an act of good faith, I shall also wipe all memory of last year, during which I made the unpopular decision to grow a handlebar moustache. Enclosed is a picture of me at the Estram-Axos Ltd. Conquistador-themed New Year's party where I am sporting the aforementioned lip-tickler, as well as a green sombrero to go with the theme. To the future, sirs!

Sincerely,
Dr. Gerald Pym

\*\*\*\*

Sept. 4
Attn: Mr. Robert Kilfoy and Associates

Hello, my name is Dr. Gerald Pym. Ever since I mysteriously awoke in one of your facilities with a severe bout of amnesia, I knew I would be a good fit for Estram-Axos Ltd., even as I was forcibly escorted out of it. I have a background in neurology and animal care. Enclosed is a résumé that I think will help you understand why your company needs me.

Sincerely,
Dr. Gerald Pym

ADAM CLARKE has a degree in English and theatre from the University of Ottawa. He lives in his hometown, St. John's.

# Unsettled

## by Annette Conway

*Cuffer Prize 2008 Honourable Mention*

Every time the 1953 Chevy hit a pothole, the bones of my bum struck the metal tailgate. I winced but couldn't move as I had my left arm around my sister, Rose, and my right arm around my brother, Thomas, to keep them from falling out. The tailgate groaned under our weight.

The truckbed behind us was packed with furniture, the picture of the Sacred Heart and fishing nets. But the smell of salt water was long gone. My bare feet hung over the back of the tailgate and I watched them become covered by a thin film of dust churned up by the truck. The dust shimmered behind us in the heavy August heat. The truck rocked and pitched from the hollows and holes in the road. I kept my brother and sister close enough so that I could keep my skirt from blowing up.

My oldest brother, Gus, was standing on the running board on Daddy's side of the truck. Daddy said he was allowed because Gus complained his legs were getting cramped sitting in the back with us. I had wanted to stand on the running board, too, but Mom said I had to mind the young ones.

I turned my head and caught a glimpse of my mother and father through a piece of cab window that was visible through the tumble of furniture. Mom was holding the new baby, George, and my younger sister, Lucy, was cuddled into Daddy's arm. I could just make out the top of her blond head.

Daddy caught my eye in the rearview mirror and winked. It made the knot in my stomach feel better. I looked at Gus watching the road ahead. He'd be the one to see St. John's first.

But I'd been the one to see St. Kyran's last.

Just yesterday we were packing up the house, the heat close against my skin, the thick smell of salt and sweet smell of juniper drifting in through the open windows. Gus was with Daddy, getting the nets from the boats. I stayed inside with Mom helping her sort through the things we would take and the things we would leave behind. The sun flickered on the harbour like silver sequins. I longed to be outside in the fresh air and not the stale dying air of the house.

"Mara, get your head out of the clouds and help me," Mom called.

I grabbed one last look at Gus down on the wharf with Daddy. They stood side by side, their backs to the house, hands in their pockets surveying the ocean. The sun was low in the sky, bleeding orange and red into the horizon. Gus and Daddy were shadows against the fading light. Long after we were all gone from the island, I would carry that picture in my mind.

"Mara – now."

I was wrapping dishes in the pages from an old Sears catalogue to ensure they would survive the trip to St. John's. We would be hours travelling on the old dirt road. The dishes had been a wedding gift from my mother's parents. They had bought them in St. John's and picked them up themselves to bring them back home for the newlyweds. Now we would be bringing them back along the same road, back to the town from which they had come.

I wrapped another teacup and glanced out the window and saw Peter out on the wharf talking to Gus and Daddy. My stomach jumped a little and I wrapped faster. I placed the wrapped dishes on top of each other in a wooden crate. I just had two more to go when in my hurry I dropped a cup. It crumbled all over the floor, in pieces too small to ever glue back together.

"Jesus, Mary and Joseph!" my mother cried. "You never broke one, did you?"

My heart sunk into my stomach. All the way from St. John's my grandparents had carried these dishes and now I had spoiled the set.

"Oh, Mom, I'm so sorry." I reached for the broom.

"Mara, you're as clumsy an old dog." She took the broom from me and batted at the bits on the floor.

"What happened?" Daddy asked as he came in.

"This one's after dropping one of my good teacups. The set's ruined now it is, ruined."

"God grant us no greater loss," Daddy said and shrugged. "I never liked those fancy Chinese cups anyway."

He winked at me while Mom was bent over with the dustpan, and gave her bum a squeeze.

"Kev, don't be at me now," she said, straightening quickly.

"Oh come on now, Trese, don't be angry. It was just an accident," he turned to me. "Mara, go on out with the boys and get a breath of air. T'is enough to suffocate you in here with the heat."

"Thanks, Daddy," I smiled.

I ran out the door and down the hill to the wharf where Gus and Peter were sat, legs hanging over the side. I slowed as I got closer, smoothed my hair out of my face and wiped at the smudges on the front of my dress. When my feet hit the wood, the boys turned at the sound.

"Hey Mara, you finished up at the house?" Gus asked.

"I just broke one of Mom's good teacups."

"That must've made her real happy," he grinned.

"It's not funny, Gus. She was some mad." I sat down beside him on the rough grey planks, carefully tucking my skirt under me.

"Don't worry, Mara, she's just worried about moving. Like everybody else."

"Yes, I suppose she is," I conceded.

I hated to admit my mother might have her own fears and worries when my own were smothering me. I shifted on the hard wood and tucked my legs under me.

The sun was sliding slowly into the ocean changing the sky from purple to lavender. Gulls weaved and dipped into the harbour.

"Did you hear that Old Man Power isn't going?" Peter asked.

"Not going?" I leaned out to look at Peter's face. "Sure, Joey said everyone's got to go."

"Well, he says he won't leave his missus here by herself." Peter shrugged.

"Sure, Mrs. Power's been dead this six month," Gus said.

"He says there'll be nobody to tend her grave," Peter said. "Dad says he's half-cracked anyway."

"I bet most people are jealous he's brave enough to stay," I said.

In the summer, after supper, the Powers would shuffle down the road, her arm linked into his.

One time, when they were walking down the road, I saw him stop by Pat Walsh's meadow, reach in beyond the fence posts and pick a bunch of daisies for her. She'd smiled the biggest smile and carried them back home.

"You know, he goes to her grave every day and puts flowers on it," Peter said. "I sees him every evening."

"How's he goin' to get by when we're all gone?" I wondered out loud.

"The same as us all," said Gus.

Silence lay across the wharf, the slapping of the waves the only sound in the still evening.

ANNETTE CONWAY was born and raised in St. John's. After studying law in Windsor, Ont., she returned to St. John's where she now practices. She lives in Torbay with her partner and son and their three dogs.

# Adventure on Signal Hill

## by Michael Nolan

*Cuffer Prize 2008 Honourable Mention*

Gerald Foley stood at the top of Signal Hill, St. John's below him, with only the wind at his ear. He wondered why, in such a beautiful spot, no one had committed suicide.

Someone may have done so, of course, and it had been hushed up by city council. Gerald imagined the mayor loading mangled bodies in the back of a truck and dumping them in the middle of the night just outside city limits, a dripping pile of corpses beyond "Welcome to Mount Pearl." The mayor would do such a thing; he was civic-minded – and the RNC would never know the difference.

Then Gerald saw his ex take a solemn plunge, his name on her lips, pinballing from rock to rock to the water below. He sighed; it would never happen. She was now with a drummer or a bass player or a rhythm section. He didn't know, but he did know, whoever it was, be it spoon-player or garage band, within a week with Alanna, he (or they) would be ready to jump. The mayor might be busy soon.

Briefly, the thought made him cheerful. He had climbed the hill to mope. Part of the problem was Alanna, but part was he had just gotten his degree: a BA (English, Hons., thesis: The Amazing Spiderman No. 31-33: A Bildungsroman) – what do you do with that? Maybe he could read "Lucky Jim" or "Catcher in the Rye" while waiting for the oil to boil into the fries or to keep from hurtling headfirst into the coffee vat during the graveyard shift. Maybe he could defend himself with a hard-covered Dickens when his co-workers, all high school dropouts, descended on him because he was so much better than they.

Then Gerald had an epiphany, a state which only the well-read achieve. If his future were fast food, why did he have to serve them here? The world was a franchise of franchises. He could wear a humiliating costume as awkwardly in London, drip sweat onto a griddle as profusely in Shanghai, shape doughnuts as doughnutty in New York as in St. John's. The world was his Big Mac.

Gerald shrugged. Mostly likely, however, Calgary was his best chance. It might not be Paris, but it could be the Promised Land. He had friends out there. He was sure he could get someone to share an apartment with him and even that wouldn't have to be for long. Jobs were falling off the trees in Calgary.

It would also be good to see a bit of the world. He'd never been off the island, never really outside of St. John's.

He would miss home though. He looked down at the city. The trees were full-green and the houses a child's crayon box beneath the deep blue early morning sky. There, on George Street, he had first kissed Alanna, the Friday night rain rivelling down her cheeks, when she had told him she'd love him forever and how much she loved music.

Above that was the Basilica, half-cleaned half-engrimed, its stately glory enscaffolded, where, when he was a boy, his parents had sent him every Sunday to Mass – and Bannerman Park, where he really went. Across from the church was The Rooms, the new arts and culture mall, all glass and sharp concrete, a little piece of Toronto disguised as tradition. There was his school, there was – someone behind him.

For about three minutes, he had been conscious of people slouching up the hill. There were two of them, both about 20 years old.

The male was about six foot, his shirt open to his naked skin, his bling jingling like wind chimes; the crotch of his jeans was bagging at his knees and the polka dots on his boxers were winking in the sun.

The female was about half a foot shorter, but bigger. She bulged. Gerald wasn't sure if she wore a halter-top or just couldn't tuck in her shirt. Her belly, diamond-studded, rolled over the top of her jeans. Both reprobates had tattooed arms and complexions as if they had been face-down in the harbour for a week.

They couldn't move fast; her jeans were so tight a sudden move might eviscerate her; his needed to be hitched up every 10 feet or so. As comic as Hell's Laurel and Hardy might seem, Gerald felt a fist twist his guts. Too many bullies, too many school days with his face pushed against the wall had trained him to fear.

Worse still, there was a third clown.

The male – Gerald christened him Legless Diamond – had on a leash a black Rottweiler, the drug-pusher's pet of choice. The dog looked trim, toothy, determined and swift. He was definitely the brains of the operation. Gerald called him Peaches.

What was this trio doing up, and up here, at this ungodly healthy hour?

Gerald spied at the group furtively, with quick peeks while he yawned or tied his shoe. He felt trapped, here at the wall around Cabot Tower, with no witnesses in sight. He might have left earlier, when he first discovered them. Now, it would be clear he would be escaping – if he could escape. He didn't want to give anyone, particularly Peaches, any offence. He stayed, perhaps because he was now a trifle paralytic. He pressed himself against the stone wall, stared at an ironically golden-shimmering downtown, and wished he'd actually gone to Mass.

He shifted his wallet to where he could quickly haul it out.

Then he heard their arrival. She was saying how "effing fantastic" it all looked. "Bet you're glad now you came up here," she said. Legless and Peaches headed toward Gerald. Gerald's spine iced.

"Hey, buddy, got a cigarette?"

Gerald didn't move. He scrutinized nothing at all even more intensely. Legless repeated himself. Gerald turned, sputtered, "S-sorry, I, ah, don't smoke," gave a sincerely apologetic smile, then gazed into his future.

There was a noise from the right. "Look at this," she insisted and Legless turned to her. The leash slackened. Peaches rammed his muzzle into Gerald's backside. Gerald squeezed his legs almost into one and he stretched himself tiptoe; he did not scream, but a silent shout echoed inside his skull. He just closed his eyes and breathed heavily, as did Peaches.

Then there was a yank on the leash and Legless said: "Hey, don't make my dog sick, buddy."

She was laughing, with a snort chorus, doubled up and staggering. She tried to speak, but couldn't. Legless looked at Gerald. Neither could define the expression of the other.

Then over the hill came the cavalry of cockroaches, a cluster of scuttling joggers in their shiny reflective flaps. They, all middle-class and middle-aged, a collection of brown wrinkles and wiry tendons, cheered themselves for reaching the top. Gerald could have kissed these spandexed John Waynes. The trio was going already. Gerald watched their shuffle. Her snigger could be heard well after they couldn't be seen.

Gerald again surveyed St. John's, his heart once more his own. He imagined three bodies bobbing in The Narrows and the mayor silently rowing towards them in the dead of night.

MICHAEL NOLAN was born in St. John's. He enjoys playing hockey, soccer and badminton. He also acts and says he "reads, but rarely writes." He has taught English literature at Memorial University.

# Snares

## by Michael Nolan

*Cuffer Prize 2008 Honourable Mention*

Night and snow were falling too early for Paul Jackson. He knew he shouldn't be in the woods now, especially not with half a flask of rum in him. He kept saying to himself, "I must be mad," but he kept moving deeper into the trees, his car and the road somewhere behind.

He wouldn't be alone here now if his Uncle Tom hadn't collapsed face-forward onto the kitchen floor. Yet Tom was the one who wanted to "have just a drop before heading off."

"Come on," he said. "It's only a flask. A baby could down that."

Paul knew his uncle thought liquor went stale if left in the bottle, but he also needed his uncle to help check for rabbits. He was the one who had urged Tom to set the traps and the 70-year-old had agreed as a favour. So Paul agreed to "just one."

One drink couldn't hurt and there was no use upsetting Tom. Paul didn't know, however, that Tom had started drinking in the morning; that was why Aunt Clare was up the shore. He forgot, too, how persuasive Tom and rum could be. Paul's first slow burning sips warmed into the next glass and the afternoon grew darker, the humour louder and the rum deeper. Then into the last glass, Paul looked up, surprised at the sky. "Come on," he said, "let's get going." Tom just slumped back. He shook his head. "No, it's too late. Go tomorrow."

Paul stood up, staggering sideways a little. "I want to go now. I'm ready. I want to go back to St. John's tomorrow."

"Well, go yourself," said Tom, half-rising and throwing out an arm.

He pitched forward, glanced off the kitchen table and landed on the floor. He stayed there, heavy and still, his breath steady, but harsh. Paul gave his uncle a dig in the side with his foot. Tom only paused his noise.

Paul stared down. Then he knelt and said into his uncle's ear: "You're a liar, old man. And you can't take a drink like a man."

Grasping onto the edge of the table, Paul heaved himself up. It took him about five minutes to get his coat, put on his shoes and make it to the door. He didn't look back.

He drove blind, cursing his uncle, damning all drunken baymen. He passed unseeing the neat lawns and the modern split-levels, the bright slant of setting sun on the curve of water and shore. He was lucky the spot in the woods was easy to find. Even so, Paul overshot the shoulder and sprayed the trees with gravel.

When he got out of the car, Paul felt the snow. It was light, but steady. Paul didn't care. He would do what he had to do. It wouldn't take that long. Yet a part of him knew he was a fool.

He was fine at first. Tom had set snares close to the road and Paul went quickly and as certainly as he could, even in the snowy dimming. The trees were not dense, the brush was low and the snow hadn't yet concealed the ground. The rabbit trails were still clear and, even if he stumbled at times, Paul found his uncle's work. There was nothing.

Yet Paul felt accomplished. There was a warmth like a liquor in his heart. He was a hunter now. It wasn't his fault he hadn't caught anything: that was Tom or just the nature of the game. Now he could talk with the boys at the office. When Mike and Steve would come in and boast about moose hunting, Paul would smile, encourage their chat, but he felt like a child. He hadn't even held a gun. They would describe their treks in the bog as if they were African safaris, their little weekend drink fests as if they were champagne orgies, and the kill as if they had faced a lion. Now he understood something of their adventure.

There was one snare left. It was further out, through a deep smother of trees, ending in a clearing. It seemed straightforward. Paul thought, "I might as well. I might've caught something." He marched forward. The sky then was snowless, the moon full upon the ground; it glittered on the trees.

As soon as Paul entered the trees, the wind rose. Within minutes, it was dark, the moon scudded by cloud, its light only flitteringly sent through branches. The snow slanted into Paul's eyes. He should have waited out the squall or even turned back. Yet he stubbornly butted forward, squinting and blinking, catching himself on branches, pushing himself through the tangles. He tripped more than once. Finally, bruised and angry, he lay where he dropped, curled his head into his knees and shut his eyes.

The storm was soon over. It was just one of those temperaments of weather. Paul got to his feet and looked around. There was a sameness of branch and trunk and snow. He might be five feet from a road or five miles to nowhere. He was tired and he wanted to go home. He tried to shove himself through where he thought he had come, but he'd get stuck. He went around the clump, but couldn't find his tracks. Then the panic began.

He rushed one way, thinking he recognized something, but he'd walk far longer than he should have. Then he'd stop, change direction, and lose himself another way. He cursed himself. He didn't want to stay the night, maybe even longer, in the woods. He could hear Mike and Steve laughing at him, mocking the great hunter. Paul hurt with despair.

He stood helpless. There was nowhere to go. The wind blew his tears across his cheek. For minutes, he gazed at nowhere, bewildered. Then he heard something that pierced his madness: low, insistent and eerie. Paul's heart was dumbfounded. It was a cry like that of a child. Paul was horrified: what could a child be doing out here now? How trapped and alone he must be.

Paul ran without thinking, following the wail through the trees. He saw nothing, only heard the fear. It rose higher and higher. Soon, the trees were scattered. The moon burst forth. Paul was in the clearing.

The shriek was unbearable. Paul couldn't stand it; he cried out. Then he saw the blood, bright red against the snow. Paul staggered nearer, drawn by horror. He was close now, almost enough to touch. Then, for a second, the crying stopped and the night was silent. A small head turned and a red eye looked into Paul's. Then the cry resumed, madly despairing and lost.

Paul turned and fled. The branches tore his clothes; he fell; he was cut. He felt nothing. It didn't take him long to batter his way through the trees, back to familiar ground and the roadway.

Inside the car, shivering, bleeding from his face and hands, Paul threw himself against the wheel and cried like a baby.

# Blue Fish

## by J.L. Scurlock

*Cuffer Prize 2008 Honourable Mention*

His history is one of the sea but the only real memories he has are those of flames.

At 6 a.m., Mr. Abbott who's almost 67, sets out for his office in his Bonavista garden. He blows on the shed door to loosen the frozen latch. Scooping yesterday's shavings off the car seat for kindling in the fire, he stokes the small potbelly. This will take the March chill off the day, he thinks.

He settles in for an afternoon of carving. It's mostly fish and boats he does but more so fish now; regardless of their size, the fish are painted blue. You ask for a salmon, trout or cod and you'll always get a blue fish, base coated in high-gloss blue marine paint. Today he's finishing a cod, a request from a mainlander, Brenda, down to visit her old stomping grounds.

The fins are already painted; they will be added later. Mrs. Abbott cuts and fashions them from margarine containers and gives them a base coat at the kitchen counter covered in newspaper. Then in the shed, Mr. Abbott speckles the fins with leftover paint people in the community donate to him.

Mr. Abbott envisions the grand fish. A strip of two-by-six, salvaged from an old stage, is sized out. Anything above where the head, back and tail will be is quickly hacked off with the hatchet. He has a pencil in his ear but the only marks that are made are invisible, etched from 54 years on the water and a good eye. He misses not a line and comes pretty near a rough shape without penetrating the skin and flesh. The rough body lies on the bench with other rough bodies, half-hewn longliners, and sloops of perfect line.

With instinct, Mr. Abbott takes a whetstone to his filleting knife. After years of splitting fish, the knife has been sharpened narrow. The seasoned metal takes fore, aft and any excess off of the wooden cod. A gnarly eye socket and saucy mouth appear. This is a well-fed fish, Mr. Abbott thinks, as he renders him as fat as the plank will allow.

The splinters need smoothing, in case a child wants to play with it, he thinks. He pulls a rum bottle that he'd minded to hide from Mrs. Abbott from behind the car seat. The men emptied it Saturday when they were over for a yarn. With a gun mitt, he grasps the neck of the bottle, scores it with a nail and gently breaks it into a box of diesel parts. Sifting through, he finds the perfect shard and wraps a rag around one side.

This is the piece of glass he'll use to smooth the skin of the fish till she's slippery. Mr. Abbott scrapes with the grain and scrapes some more. This is the longest part to making a fish, but it isn't tedium. The relaxing rhythm puts him back in time. He remembers how, as a boy, he'd walk five miles to Lance's Cove in the pitch dark. He recollects the birds, and the smells of being on the water. Most of all, he remembers fish, and lots of it.

This morning he remembers when his own children first came out on the water, despite Mrs. Abbott's protestation. No harm though, for they were just along for the ride, and the sea was good that morning. There was excitement in the children's eyes at their initiation. They nattered back at the gulls. The nets were full and the boat dipped to welcome the load. The sun rose to warm their small, uncomplaining hands.

Not a whimper was heard that morning, and Mr. Abbott recalls his pride and hopes for his children. He looked at the faces of his youngsters and saw his and Mrs. Abbott's faces and all their families in them. He told them that they were healthy and strong and fortunate to live such a bountiful existence. The kids laughed and hooked a brazen sculpin back over the gunnel. Perhaps they're not quite old enough to heed yet, he thought.

Mr. Abbott was nicked and woken by the glass. He'd never cut himself before carving fish. He looked at the droplet of blood on the glass and trusted that it was sterilized by the rum. He thought of the rum drinkers on Saturday.

They talked about all the young folk who had moved off to the mainland because there were no fish, and how those still around were talking of going, too.

He thought of his own children and grandchildren who had hated to leave but had to. There were plenty of tears on their departure. He had to give them his blessings though; he always wanted what was best for them.

He pressed his handkerchief onto his cut and looked out the window. He remembered draggers in the distance, ripping up the ocean floor. There weren't any boats on the horizon today though, nor any in the bay.

He saw Mrs. Abbott waving in the kitchen window. It surely couldn't be suppertime yet, he thought. She was pointing to the road. A shiny rent-a-car pulled into their lane. It was the mainlander who had done well in sales in "Aww-de-wa," as she'd say.

The mainlander couldn't figure the bolt on the gate, so she struggled over the fence. At that, her pumps gave way as she slipped on the lightly dusted ice. A few burrs left over from last summer clung to her slacks. She let out a few oaths scanning around to see if anyone had witnessed her folly, then began to pick the burrs off.

Mr. Abbott looked down at his fish and then to the window. Again at the fish, and its wooden eye stared back. He contemplated how his true life, and his recollections of it, are at odds.

He smoothed the fish's slippery finless skin, minding not to bloody her. For a moment he thought he felt her writhing body wrestle at his clutch.

The mainlander was on the stoop and rattling at the frozen latch. Mr. Abbott imagined his children and hoped they hadn't sold out to something bigger and better. The mainlander was knocking now and calling for him. He looked at his fish cradled in his unbloodied hand.

The mainlander knocked some more.

"Are you in there Mr. Abbott?"

He donned his gun mitt.

"Mr. Abbott, it's Brenda from AWW-DE-WA ..."

Mr. Abbott lifted the lid of the stove and threw the fish into the fire. At first she sang, then she whined and cracked in the heat, her skin soiled and sooty. She exploded in a shower of flankers just as the mainlander pushed open the door.

"Mr. Abbott ..."

"No fish today," said Mr. Abbott, "no fish today."

J.L. SCURLOCK has been writing short, poetic, and dramatic fiction for over 10 years. She has produced several of her stage and screen scripts and has studied and taught creative writing. She is also an artist and art teacher who lives and works out of St. John's and Bristol's Hope, Conception Bay.

# Requiem for Monica

## by Deborah Whelan

*Cuffer Prize 2008 Honourable Mention*

I am old, but my memory serves me well, and before I die I want the truth to be known. I remember that early winter morning in our old saltbox in King's Point as if it were yesterday. As plain as day, I can see Monica shivering in her flannel nightdress as we press our faces to the grate in our bedroom floor, billows of heat rising up from the kitchen stove below.

"Mom must be out to the henhouse," Monica says, "Do you think she left some rolled oats for us? Let's go down and see, Annie. I'm starving."

The kitchen table is empty except for the kerosene lamp. Mom has certainly had an early start, with a large bowl of bread dough wrapped in tablecloths rising on the wooden bench near the cast iron stove. Bright rays of sunshine streak the walls, the only sound the tick-tock of the clock. Everything is neat and clean. Mom likes it that way.

Standing on tiptoe to see out the windows, we can see Mom's footprints leading far across the snowy field to the barn.

"She'll be gone for too long. I'm so hungry. Let's find something to eat." Monica reaches to open the cupboard and then stops suddenly, her brown eyes like saucers in her thin face. "I know what we can have. Let's make toutons."

"We're not allowed. We'll get a lacin'," I protest, frowning at my older sister. Only one year younger at seven, I feel older, more responsible. "And anyway, we don't know how, and anyhow Mom don't want us touchin' the dough, you know that."

"But, Annie, Dad made me promise before he left to try and eat more so I can get strong again." Her pale cheeks dimple as she smiles at me. "Come and help me and we'll just make little buns and roast them on the stove. We'll make enough for Mom, too. I'll bet she'll be starved when she finishes with the cows and she'll be glad to have some."

The bench is at the perfect height as we pull the cloths off the pan. The bread is rounded and high, spilling over the top as we wrestle with it, trying our best to punch it down as we'd watched Mom do many times.

"We need some flour to put on our hands so the dough won't stick to us," I explain, climbing on a chair to reach the flour can on the top shelf. It tips and spills to the floor, sending clouds of flour through the air.

"Annie, we have to clean this up before Mom gets back ... but first, let's make some buns, and while they're roasting, we'll sweep this all up." Monica bends her little head to the side, troubled. "Do you think she'll be mad at us? I don't want to make her mad again."

I should have stopped her then. I have wished so many times that I had stopped her then. But I am caught up in the excitement, and all I say is, "Let's get started."

Our heads bend to our task, and we pull and pat and shape, sliding happily in our vamps between the bench and the stove. Soon rows of crooked little dough balls puff up on the dampers. The stove is hot indeed, especially the front dampers where the fire is lit just underneath. The smell of scorched bread fills the kitchen.

Monica looks at me. "Get the turner so we can turn them over. They'll be so good with some molasses, just like toutons."

But they are stuck to the stove; the turner doesn't help. We take turns scraping at them but just break off the tops and leave the burning bottoms there. I manage to lift off three little pieces intact when the door opens into the porch. Cold air seeps in. Mom is back from the barn.

I watch through the half-opened kitchen door as she lays a bucket of water on the shelf below the window, her old plaid coat stuck with bits of hay, her face red from the cold. She stops and frowns as she sniffs the air.

In two steps, Mom pushes open the door and is in the kitchen, her jaw dropping as she views the scene before her through the smoke: the spilled flour, the pan of flattened dough, the burnt offerings covering her stove.

"What in God's name are you up to?"

She grabs a piece of firewood from the wood box and strikes me across the back. My fear is greater than the pain as I run for the stairs, hearing Monica's little voice, soft and trembling, say, "It's not her fault, Mom, don't hurt Annie, Mom, OK?"

"You sleeveen! What did I ever do to deserve a punishment from God like you? You're nothing but trouble. You think you're going to get away with this? Your father's not here now for you to make eyes at him. Pretending you're sick to get his attention. I'll show you."

I hear the thump of the piece of wood again and again and I hear Monica scream. I run back to the kitchen doorway. Monica is lying on the floor, still and white. Mom is kneeling next to her, still holding the stick of wood.

"Monica has taken sick again. She's fainted." Mom throws the wood into the stove and then picks up Monica and carries her up the stairs. I follow behind her and stand cautiously beside the bedroom door as Mom lays her on our bed and pulls the quilt around her.

"Go downstairs and clean up your mess." Mom looked at me, her eyes cold. "She should have stayed in bed instead of running around getting overheated. Now she's going to be sick again. God in Heaven, is there ever a minute of peace with you two?"

Later, when Mom goes to bring in more wood for the stove, I climb the stairs and lay down next to Monica. I put cold cloths on her forehead; I sing her favourite songs, hoping to wake her. But she lies very still and quiet.

That night, with my arms around her, Monica dies. From pneumonia, Mom tells everyone; poor Monica's been sickly for a long time. The next day, Aunt Nora comes over to help Mom wash and dress her, but Mom doesn't want help. She says she wants to be alone this last time with her baby. She brushes and braids Monica's dark, curly hair and dresses her in the yellow dress that Grandma had made for her eighth birthday.

Dad would have said she looked as pretty as a picture, except that he is so far away in the lumber camps he won't know that she's gone until it's too late to kiss her goodbye.

It'll be too late then to see the ugly bruises on her back or the dent in the back of her head, well hidden by Mom's clever coil of braids.

DEBORAH WHELAN is from the Port au Port Peninsula but lives in Mount Pearl, where she enjoys writing as "the great escape." She is married and has three children.

# The Stick Shift
## by Owen Whelan

*Cuffer Prize 2008 Honourable Mention*

When Ralph drops by Pearl's place to pick her up, she's putting up curtain rods, standing on a chair by the window, holding a screwdriver.

"I'll do that for you when we come back," he says.

"I was standing here wondering how I'd ever get it done without you."

He ignores the comment. Time has changed nothing, he's thinking, she's as touchy as ever.

She puts away the screwdriver, finds a jacket and follows him out. When she sees the car she laughs.

"Bright red! Sports model! That car's not you."

"No," Ralph says, "it's a Nissan Maxa hatchback, 6-speed standard."

"Going back to being a teenager?"

"No, ahead, to two-bucks-a-litre gas."

When you start a Sunday afternoon drive on the Irish Loop, you sooner or later reach a point where it's just as well to keep on going as turn around. Somewhere on the shore that happens, so they have a lunch in Trepassey and come back through St. Mary's Bay. They enjoy the scenery, talk about old times, how communities are changing and what she plans to do now she's back home, retired. They have some long silent stretches.

Ralph is wondering what his future might be if he plays his cards right, if he's a bit more sensitive. Maybe, he thinks, she ...

Pearl interrupts his thoughts.

"Let me drive the Salmonier Line? I haven't done it in years."

He's reluctant to give her the wheel, but since Sunday suppertime is light traffic, he pulls in on a straight stretch near the Salmonier River bridge, gets out and holds the door while she comes around. She adjusts the seat, straps herself in, moves the mirrors to suit.

"Take it easy now," he says.

"You can't go for long without being sexist. Can you? Would you tell any of your male friends to take it easy? Or would you hold the door for any of them?"

Ralph doesn't answer.

The Salmonier Line links St. Mary's Bay to Conception Bay and crosses the Trans-Canada Highway near Holyrood. The first three Ks are little slopes and gentle curves along the riverbank. The next three are a climb up the Back River Hill to the height of land. Pearl reaches 140 before having to slow for a Rav4 coming from The Wilds golf club on top of the hill.

"Two guys heading back to town after a day of golf," Ralph says in an attempt to slow her down.

"Yes, back to the wives who were caring for their children all day."

"Don't blame me," he says.

The Maxa is registered for 220 but Ralph never expected to do more than half that. He tries not to look at the speedometer as she passes the Rav4, thinking it's better not to know, and he won't say anything even if it kills him. In one breath he's praying for some traffic to rein her in, and in the next for none to get in her way. He concentrates on the landscape.

The Line was once part of the main route from the U.S. navy base at Argentia to St. John's. There's an old story that the Americans built curves into it to prevent its being bombed in a straight line. Ralph believes that's a myth. It's more likely, he thinks, that early travellers stuck to the driest route, going around the ponds and marshes, and staying high on the riverbanks. The present-day curves, dips and little blind hills are the result.

There's a blind hill and a straight stretch into a sharp curve near Deer Park. Pearl gears down to fourth to pass a Ford Escape and then changes back to fifth. They pass the nature park and the old prison camp so fast, Ralph doesn't have time to tell her that Deer Park is now one of the larger summer settlements on the Avalon, or that the nature park is a wonderful place for an afternoon visit, or that the prison camp is now closed.

He tries to relax, telling himself he'll get through this. He notices that she's good at what she's doing even though she hasn't been within the speed limit since they left the bridge. She has the engine anywhere from a satisfying rumble to an excited scream as she goes through the gears, and she uses each one to its maximum. He's amazed at how she doesn't wander on the curves.

Some people, Ralph has found, when they drive standard, will jerk you all over the place, just about give you whiplash. He's surprised she's not like that. At times she's holding the gearshift firmly, pushing and pulling it as if she's saying, "You're going there, whether you want to or not." Then suddenly she's gentle, holding it between thumb and fingers, moving it smoothly to where she wants it.

She's right, Ralph thinks, I am sexist. But it was so innocent, the curtain rod thing; she should have ignored that. And the holding doors, well. ... And the dig about the car, how it's not me; that wasn't fair. She's got nearly as much mileage as I have; though, like they say in real estate, she shows well.

Father Duffy's Well is a monument to a priest who led a bunch of lawbreakers along this trail back in the 1830s. He struck a boulder with his staff and brought forth water. The highway along here is a series of awkward curves and dips by a couple of ponds on either side of the road. Pearl is going so fast Ralph expects the worst. He hangs onto his seat and they come out the other side OK. Nearing the end now, he feels like that last few minutes when a plane is landing in turbulence, when you stare out the window trying to blot out reality.

Pearl has her foot to the floor on a straight level stretch by Bermuda Lake when a moose appears on the pavement ahead. It wasn't there and then it was. Ralph presses his two feet into the floor, and grabs the dash. She touches the brake for the first time since they left the bridge, gears down, and brings the car to a stop, tight to the moose's ass.

Ralph is thinking, Mr. Moose, we're both crazy to be where we are and you have a choice: kick a red hatchback into the scrapyard or go on into the trees. The moose opts for the forest.

Pearl takes off again as if she meets incidents like this every day and does the last five Ks to the TCH like she's making up time in a Targa rally. She pulls in on a parking lot near the main highway, and Ralph gets out. He rushes up a path into the trees to get rid of some Trepassey tea. When he comes back she's still in the driver's seat, with her window down.

"You can drive now," she says.

He moves away from the door to let her out. She looks at him and smiles.

And Ralph is thinking, Pearl, you're right, this car is not me.

But he doesn't tell her that.

OWEN WHELAN was born in Riverhead, St. Mary's Bay and lives in St. John's. A retired construction worker and teacher, he enjoys painting and writing.

# Friday Night

## by Richard Barnes

I was 14 in 1968, and every Friday night, I went to the dairy at 6 o'clock to meet my buddy, Conk. The "dairy" was the plant where milk collected from local dairy farmers was pasteurized and packaged for sale in the new square containers. Conk changed into his jeans from his white shirt, pants and rubber boots and punched out his time card. We went to a grease joint for fish and chips. A little farther west was Nancy's, where we played pool. Monday morning was far away, and homework was put off until Sunday. Anything was possible on Friday night.

"Seen Christina today. She's looking good." Conk said, patting the pocket where the striped high ball would go. "Her father still won't let her go out on a date, though, and she's 17, now!"

Christina Fowloe lived just across the road from the dairy. I'd seen her walk by the loading bay on her way to the counter to buy milk. Sometimes she stopped to have a cigarette with Conk.

Cigarette burning between his lips, Conk squinted his eye as he lined up his shot. "Christina said Wints is gone completely blind. Diabetes got into his other eye." Another high ball sunk. He chalked the tip of his cue. "Wints" was Winston Fowloe, Christina's dad.

One night I showed up at the dairy to find Conk standing in a huge stainless steel vat with a scrubbing brush.

"I can't go out, Dick. I'm working an extra shift tonight. They want to load the trucks tonight so they are ready to roll first thing in the morning."

"Bummer. Well, it's extra money though."

"That's what it's all about. Hey, take two quarts of fresh chocolate over to Christina, will you?"

I walked over to Christina's with the chocolate milk. She answered the door. She had straight, shiny dark hair, almond-shaped eyes with black pupils, full breasts and long legs. Her skin was the colour of honey.

"Hi! Chocolate milk from Henry?"

"That's right. Fresh from the vat. Conk, er, Henry had to work tonight so he asked me to deliver it."

"Thanks so much."

"Who's that?" Wints bellowed from the kitchen.

"Henry's friend, Dick, with chocolate milk."

"Tell him to come in."

I entered the bright, spotless kitchen. Wints was shuffling a deck of cards, staring straight ahead. Well, not really staring, but his dark eyes were aimed straight ahead. Wints had the same almond-shaped eyes as his daughter, the same honey-coloured skin. His hands looked huge and his mouth was small, round and pulled to one side; unlike Christina's, which was wide and full of bright, even teeth.

"What are you doing on Friday night?"

"Well, I was going to play pool with my buddy Henry, but he has to work."

"What about a hand of crib?"

I looked at Christina. She said, "You have to play the two of us. I help Dad with his cards."

"Sure," I said.

Wints was in a chair at one end of the table. At the sides were padded benches like a restaurant booth. Christina slid along the right-hand bench and sat next to Wints. To my delight, she patted the bench next to her. I slid in next to Christina.

Wints shuffled the cards with his left hand into his right, then took the deck in his left hand and dealt them out with the right, the cards landing neatly in two piles of six for each of us. He laid the deck on the table. I cut the cards and he turned up the eight of hearts.

"Eight of hearts, Daddy."

I laid the seven of hearts. "Fifteen for two."

Christina whispered in her father's ear. He laid the nine of hearts. "7-8-9 for three."

Christina smiled at me and pegged her father's score. While we played, Wints talked.

"One Friday night, not long after I got out of the army, I was working at the Foundry and a couple of the boys dragged me down to the Porthole Lounge after work. We sat at a table and drank beer all night. Around midnight, I said goodnight to the boys, who were singing it up at the table, and made my way out the door. On the street, two American sailors walked up to me. One was a great big goon, and the other was short and stout like a puncheon.

"I still had my lunch box with me. 'What you got there, Chink?' the big one said.

"'Chink,' he called me, because of my eyes. I heard that before, though, an' I wouldn't get into a fight over that, but those two meant to do me harm. The big one kept inching toward me, and the puncheon kept twisting his fat head to see if anyone else was around.

"'What's in the lunchbox, Chink?' he says. They would've got 'Chink' if they had been where I was in K'rea. The K'reans were tough as nails, an' then the Chinese got into it. They were some soldiers, b'y. The Chinese travelled by night, over the worst kind of country, too, mountains and everything. Walked all night, and slept during the day — if they got any sleep at all. They'd pop up way behind the lines and drive back our units before we knew what hit us."

I tallied up my cards and Christina counted Wints's. I shuffled the cards and spun out new hands.

"Napalm was only new then, and the Americans dumped hundreds of thousands of tons of it on K'rea. Burned villages full of people, towns, factories, everything. They were going to use atomic bombs, too, 'cause they knew they couldn't drive the Chinese out. Fifteen for two. Anyway, the big one was looking at my lunch tin — I had a big black one with a rounded lid.

"'Wassin the lunchbox?' he says, edging closer.

"'Two-dozen leechee nuts for me mother,' I said, holding up the lunchbox a bit. I can still see the two of them grinning, their faces glowing white under the streetlight by the Porthole.

"'Lemme see.' The big one made a grab for the lunch tin. I let him see it all right. I clocked him over the eye with it, and before the smile was gone off the puncheon, I drove my left fist into his teeth. And I ran. I don't think the big one got up, and I could hear the little puncheon bawling out for help and swearing."

Christina helped Wints gather the cards. He did the left hand shuffle again.

"I didn't stop running until I reached Waterford Bridge. I got under the old bridge and sat on the concrete footing, pulled off my boots and socks, and soaked my feet in the cool water. I opened my lunch tin. In a Mammy's bread bag, I had 24 stove bolts I took from the Foundry, and a boloney sandwich left over from lunch. I never tasted anything better in my life.

"Fifteen for two."

"21 for two…"

RICHARD (RICK) BARNES recently retired from CBC Television where, as a producer, he toiled in the world of factual entertainment. He has been writing fiction and poetry all his life and has been published in The Telegram and Downhome magazine.

# The Manor

## by Gerard Collins

"Where is he?"

"Upstairs," she half-whispered. "You'll wake him if you're not careful."

"Sorry." Eva tossed her coat across the banister and reached behind to shut the door. It still rattled slightly as it closed.

*She tries, God love 'er.* Sarah could only shake her head. Her older sister wasn't exactly the tiptoeing type.

"Coffee?"

"Love some." Eva followed her into the kitchen, scanning the walls and ceiling, seeming to take note of every cobweb and pockmark.

"My God, Sarah, they've been in this house as long as I've been alive."

"Same year you were born. Yes, I know the story."

Sitting at the table, Eva seemed to swallow some words behind her red-lipsticked mouth as Sarah boiled the kettle and set the coffee pot brewing. "The old garden's seen some hard times. I used to always love looking at it from this spot."

"You could look at it some more if you'd move back here."

"Back here? I'd have to be pretty old and senile to do that."

Sarah shot her a sarcastic look.

"Oh." Eva brought her hands to her face, feigning embarrassment. "I can't believe I just said that."

"So, now that you've said it – what *are* we going to do with him?"

Sarah motioned her head upwards, eyes raised to the ceiling.

"Ah, yes, his holiness. Lord of the manor."

"He's been Lord of this manor for a long time."

"Mom always knew what to do with him." Eva's eyes filled with tears, which she wiped away with elaborate casualness.

"She's not here, though."

"I know that. Don't you think I know that? Jesus, Sarah. I wasn't saying we should wake her from the dead to ask what to do with her poor, sick husband."

"I didn't mean it like that." Sarah drew in a deep breath. Everything was a negotiation with Eva. "I mean that she raised us to, hopefully, know what to do in this situation."

"Well, you're right about that. There's only one thing to be done, and the sooner we sign the papers and get him into Breezy Manor the sooner we can all get a good night's sleep."

"I'm the one who lives here."

"So I should feel guilty because I live so far away? Got it easy, yessir. Good ol' Eva's got 'er knocked up there in the big city. Don't have to worry about nudding."

"I never said that."

"No, but you implied it."

Sarah closed her eyes and gazed out at the garden, thinking that the petunias were wilting, along with everything else. That backyard had been her mother's pride and joy. "The best little garden on Forest Road," she used to say, to which her father would reply, "Never mind Forest Road. Best in all of Newfoundland! You think the Crosbies or Murphys have a backyard like ours?" Of course, her mother agreed with him.

"What are you thinking?"

Eva's voice brought Sarah back to the moment. She shook her head slightly to clear out the cobwebs. "I'm thinking it's too bad things have to go this way."

The elder sister laid her hand atop the younger one's, squeezing it tenderly. "I know what you mean. But it always does. Some day this will be me and you, and somebody will have to figure out what to do with this big old mansion."

"We'll deal with it when the time comes, I suppose."

"For now, though, we deal with this."

Sarah was afraid of those words from her sister. Eva had always been the business side of the two. She knew what to do and wasn't afraid to carry it out. Or, if she was, she did it anyway. "Deal how?"

"Bring our father to a place where people can take care of him properly."

Sarah felt tears welling in her eyes. She let go of Eva's hand in order to wipe them away. "I'm just not sure, Eva."

"What's to be sure about?"

"Anything. This. Doesn't it affect you at all?"

"Of course it does. But I'm realistic enough to know he's a sick old man, and no matter how much you or I might love him, we're not equipped to give him the 24/7 care that a man in his condition needs. My God, you told me on the phone he almost died last week."

"He woke up and didn't know where he was. Started wandering around, turning on lights and the stove burners."

"If that wouldn't scare the bejesus out of anyone –"

"When I got up to check on him, he was yellin' out, '*Goddamn them all!*' "

"Was he hallucinating about the war or singing Stan Rogers?" Eva smiled wryly, the familiar twinkle in her eye for the first time since she'd come home.

Sarah laughed in spite of herself. "Eva! You're shockin'. Making fun of a frail, old man!"

"Hey, don't tell me he wouldn't do the same thing. There wasn't a harder ticket around than our old man."

"Still," said Sarah. "He's earned some respect."

Eva's face hardened, but her eyes suddenly softened as if she might cry. The contrast was frightening to the younger sister. "Respect?" She laughed sarcastically. "Yeah, sure. Respect. I could tell a few things, but I won't since you're still so in love with him."

"What did he ever do to you?"

Eva licked her red lips and straightened her back. "Never mind. We've got to decide."

"Coffee first." Sarah got up to fix the refreshments and brought them to the table on a silver tray, her hands trembling so that the silver spoons rattled.

"What do you say, Sis?" Eva looked at her with those business-blue eyes of hers, and Sarah knew it was coming to an end. All of it. Everything her parents had ever had and worked for. Everything she had so fearfully clung to. Everything Eva had so gallantly despised.

"I don't know what to say. If I just say yes –"

"The nightmare will be over. You can sleep at night. You can visit him in the evenings after work. There'll be people there to take good care of him."

"Don't you care about him at all?"

Eva drew back in her chair as if she'd been face-slapped. "It's not about that. This is about doing the right thing."

"Tell me what *is* the right thing, Eva. Because it's not that easy for me. Maybe for you, but not me."

Eva just shook her head. "It's never easy, Sarah. It'll never be easy. It'll always be the hardest goddamn thing you ever did. It'll rip your heart out every single time, whether it's this or a funeral or something else. But you still have to deal with it." She laid her hand atop her sister's again, fixing her cold blue eyes upon her. "*We* have to."

Sarah slouched forward until her forehead nearly touched the doily on the table in front of her. Thinking better of it, she looked up and saw the pain etched in her sister's features. It was like looking into a mirror.

"All right," she said in a faraway voice that she couldn't swear was hers.

GERARD COLLINS has published in various literary journals and has won several provincial arts and letters prizes, including in 2006, 2007 and 2008. He has also won the Percy Janes First Novel Award and is now working on both a new gothic novel and a short-story collection called "Moonlight Sketches."

# Under the Flake

## by Jim Combden

A boy not in the skiff with his father roamed beaches under flakes. Skipping rocks, sailing boats and trapping birds. Often a laying pullet rather than a beach bird would be snapped between two rusty steel jaws. Isaac got no fishing experience until his mother remarried, when Isaac was 13. Until then, he was a beachcomber.

Skipping rocks required a flexible wrist, a keen eye, and excellent balance. The aim was to start the stone skipping as soon as it hit the water. This took an unlimited supply of flat rocks. Over five years, 50 per cent of Little Harbour's beach was skipped into the ocean.

Isaac competed in skipping contests. A champion was declared every week, with Stan, Melvin and Wendell wearing invisible crowns several times before August's end. No ribbons or trophies, just a slap on the back and a dozen flat rocks, with the satisfaction of knowing you could skip a stone to the Funks.

Saltwater ponds below the flakes had a permanent supply of tiny fish, about two inches long. Darnybats, the local name. A cocktail fruit tin trapped the fish, which were immediately transferred to the boat's stomach for shipment to an imaginary country. Boys became fishermen, crossing rough seas to deliver a hundred barrels of fresh snails, starfish and crabs.

Little white sails, cut from an old pillowcase, adorned crude boats chopped from planks and slabs. Tiny fish, 10 to a boat, swelled to thousands with a sprinkle of imagination. Unfortunately, these little creatures died when removed from their natural habitat. Isaac watched tiny mouths gasping for air, but his heart was as cold as the ocean.

Traps offered daily surprises. There was the risk of trapping a rooster, hen or cat, creating a civil war. Stan and Isaac laid fox traps with teeth that snapped off wings, legs, necks and fingers. The initial inspection revealed the toes of Aunt Ivy's red pullet attached to the plate. The bird staggered toward home. Flinging the trap into the harbour, two criminals sneaked away under the code of silence.

Grandmother said, "A still tongue makes a wise head." In this case, two still tongues would save two heads.

"Don't say a word," whispered Stan, putting a forefinger to his lips. Like thieves, they slipped around the shore and approached their homes from a direction not visible through Aunt Ivy's kitchen window. If the hen hopped home before Isaac did, he became the prime suspect.

Hurricane Ivy hit with vengeance. "Dem boys got da leg cut off me best laying hen. I knows 'tis them, they're forever in the landwash. They'll have to pay for that lovely pullet." Froth flew from Ivy's lips, as she raged over the rocks to grandmother's bridge. Few warriors faced this fury, and those who tried had eyeballs, necks and faces scratched and clawed. Ivy was known to aim her boot, with great accuracy, toward the most sensitive parts of the anatomy.

Ivy reached her climax as she planted her shoe on the bridge. "Can't let ya hens out," she blared, "my poor, legless hen, my favourite. No more brown eggs, lays all year, what a sin." She dabbed her eyes with the hem of her apron.

Gran, in her floor-length black dress, buttoned to her chin, silver brooch glittering on her bosom, was greeted by a shower of accusations. Gran blinked, blew on her wire-rimmed glasses, and rubbed the lenses with a wrinkled blue handkerchief she kept tucked in her sleeve. "What is da trouble?" Gran was a cool dude, not easily rattled. She knew a volcano would erupt on the room some day. A footless hen had triggered that eruption.

"Is 'e in the house?" demanded Aunt Ivy, cuddling her precious pullet. A piece of red cloth hung from where a foot once was. "I wants to talk to that boy."

"What boy?" asked Lilly, her hands on her hips, peering over her glasses, as if to challenge. "Go fer ya guns."

Ivy sneered. "You know what boy – only one would do da like a that, da same one who tied da birch rind on da cat's tail … drove poor Lizzy nearly off her 'ed. Poor cat went crazy … bolted like lightning up da flagpole … never seen since." She glanced at the hen, touched her comb. "Is 'e in da house?"

Isaac cowered under a punt's snail in his uncle's store. He did not stir until the storm changed course. Lilly would hold the fort and survive the hurricane. Stan cowered under a ballast-bed below the Nap.

Ivy did not retreat. "That boy should be in reform school," she sputtered. Not having a father gave people the gall to condemn a boy to rough justice in a shabby St. John's building where inmates were whipped and forced to scrub concrete floors. Isaac heard stories of ears tortured with pliers, heads pressed into toilet bowls, and having to hold a 50-pound bag of sand over your head.

But a legless hen could not convict. Without an eyewitness, or the bloody trap, Hurricane Ivy could do little damage. "Did Isaac do that?" she squealed, her eyes afire with murder. If he were present, his eyes might have been gouged.

Grandmother peered through her cataracts. She sniffed, blinked and folded her hands. "What are you saying?" Ivy was up against a stubborn woman. Lilly would bat her grandchild across the head and send him to bed without supper, if he were guilty; but she would defend him to the death if the evidence was as flimsy as a pullet with one foot. Ivy would not overcome Lilly Mary.

"'E's as guilty as sin," added Ivy, pushing the severed foot an inch from Lilly's nose. No hen was ever broodier than this intruder. "That trap come from Skipper Garge's store, plain as da nose on ya face, da young snot." She bivvered with revenge.

Gran licked her lips. Ivy stepped backwards. "Da best t'ing you can do is go on home. You can't say Isaac did dis ... there's traps all over the beach. Go home and soak ya head in water ... you have no proof. Did your boy break da winder in Tite's stage? He was seen on da premises, but I can't say da boy is guilty." Daggers protruding from Gran's eyes froze Ivy in her tracks. The battle lost, Ivy turned and strutted away like a pissed-off rooster.

Grandmother would not convict her boy on circumstantial evidence. She knew he was involved, but tradition demanded she defend her own. At duckish, Isaac crept from his bunker, and crawled into the kitchen. Gran shot him a look that could kill a dogfish.

Lilly was an honorable woman, and when her spring's brood of chicks was hatched, she picked out a beautiful red one and ordered Isaac to take it to her neighbour. Ivy accepted the bird without comment, but Isaac told his Gran Ivy gave him a bun and a hug. Gran knew the difference, but remained silent. That night, Isaac prayed that the latest addition to Ivy's family would turn out to be a rooster.

JIM COMBDEN is a retired teacher living in Badger's Quay. He taught literature for 30 years but now focuses on his own wordcraft, from poetry to commentary. His short story in this collection is part of a larger work he is working on about growing up in Barr'd Islands, Fogo Island.

# The Purse

## by Mark Hoffe

It was bone-white leather with a tassel zipper and it hung from her smooth, dimpled shoulder like a half-moon dangling from some high-fashion heaven. She paid $200 minus a penny for it, plus tax. She grabbed it for every excursion, always kept it within reach, coddled it on her lap when she was down in the dumps. She would dig past her daily planner and wallet, search through her copious collection of lip gloss, mascara, tampons, nail files, eyebrow brushes and the abundant other bric-a-brac that kept her beauty in tune with the fashion glossies.

She always remembered the day she bought it, thanks to the hefty tip left by a drunken table of 15 itinerant oil industry bigwigs. She relished the memory of the boutique owner's magic words:

"It's one of a kind."

She never thought she would lose it.

She never did.

It just vanished into thin air.

\* \* \*

She blurted a four-letter word and scrambled out of bed. Topless and frazzled, lips stained from a late-night rendezvous with a bottle of Chilean Shiraz, she scurried to the bathroom, guts churning.

"Mick, babe, get up!" she yelled. "I'm late!"

She leaned into her new oval mirror, meticulously plucking microscopic eyebrow hairs with refined precision.

Mick crawled out of bed, holding his pounding head, and scuffed his way to the bathroom.

"You know," mused Mick, "that shower curtain is pure downtown St. John's. Orange polka dots, blue polka dots, green polka dots, red polka dots. There's even a purple polka dot. All the colours of the big ramshackle rows of houses are there."

"I know what it looks like, Mick," she said, jumping into the shower. "I bought the thing."

"I love this city," continued Mick. "We might be the national punch line, but we got charm. Charm goes a long way."

"Go make some coffee," she suggested.

"I don't think we have time for coffee, Jess." Mick pulled the curtain back a little, watching the water trickle along her slim, sexy body. Her silver toe ring shimmered like a deep-sea treasure.

\*\*\*

"It's got to be in the house somewhere," said Mick, turning the corner onto Water Street.

"I'm telling you, Mick, it's gone. Vanished. Got it?"
Mick brought the car to an abrupt double park and gave the finger to the man honking behind him. The engine hissed and sputtered.

"Listen, Jess. Don't worry. I'll find the purse. I'm sure you just took it upstairs or threw it in a closet or something. For all we know, you did a little sleep walking and put it in the fridge."

Jess, irritated, slammed the door and darted across the street towards the restaurant.

"I was just trying to comfort you!" bellowed Mick. "It's only a purse!"

\*\*\*

A crumpled note bearing the familiar chicken scratches of her boss was waiting for Jess on the cash register. She had to dust all the ketchup bottles, organize all the brunch jam packets and soak all the mugs in bleach.

"Freak," she muttered, and threw the note into the waste basket. She searched the cash area, hoping she might have left the purse at work the night before. Nothing.

\*\*\*

Mick removed his sneakers and headed straight for the fridge. Nothing but some cranberry juice, dry moldy bagels, roasted red pepper hummus two days past its expiration date and three cold beers. He cracked a beer to take the edge off and continued his investigation.

Ten minutes later, dizzy from a prolonged search under, behind and between the cushions of the couches and chairs, richer by 75 cents and holding a dusty black bra, Mick chugged the remainder of his beer and plopped down on the couch for a rest.

Jess kicked open the swing door and dropped the last of the dirty plates into the overflowing dish bin.

"Hurry up and get this thing cleaned out," she commanded the sweat-soaked dishwasher before storming back into the empty, post-lunch rush dining area.

Jess took a sip of her warm diet cola, snatched her emergency bag of supplies from behind the stereo system and ran to the bathroom. Gazing into her two swollen, red eyes welling with tears, she tried to steady her trembling hand and apply a fresh coat of mascara.

"C'mon, Jess," urged Mick. "We've been up for over 30 hours and this is our only day off. If we couldn't find it inside the house, there's no chance we're gonna find it out here."

Frustration and fatigue were forcing Jess and Mick towards the point of delirium. Sweating and sun-burnt, their skin red as boiled lobster shells, they had scoured the neighbourhood, peeked over fences into backyard lawns and gardens, rummaged through dumpsters, crawled through tall grass, lodged miniscule shards of glass and tiny pebbles into various areas of their hands and knees. Jess collapsed onto the curb, dropped her face into her hands and began to sob like a little girl.

"That's it," she muttered. "I give up."

"Let's get some lunch," said Mick, helping her up.

They locked hands and trudged down the hill towards Duckworth Street.

"What do you feel like?" asked Mick.

"Right now I feel like dying."

"No, I mean what do you want to eat?"

"Let's try the new vegetarian place. I hear they have an awesome spinach melt on house-baked spelt and a wonderful selection of soups."

"Do you know you sound like a waitress when you talk about food?"

Jess chuckled and gave Mick a gentle punch in the arm.

\*\*\*

As they turned the corner onto Duckworth Street, Mick felt Jess's hand stiffen. She stopped dead in her tracks.

"What's wrong?" asked Mick.

"Look over there. See her?"

"Who?"

"That woman in the red dress."

"What about her?"

Before Mick could get a proper handle on the situation, Jess broke free and darted through the screeching, halting, honking traffic.

"Give it back, you bitch!"

"Are you crazy?" blurted the woman, startled, backing away from Jess.

"Jess!" shouted Mick.

Jess charged the woman, making bestial yanks at the purse, hauling the woman to the ground as she shrieked and kicked, striking Jess in the temple with the pointed toe of her black leather high heels. Jess swirled and staggered, caught her balance and fell upon her with renewed vigour.

\*\*\*

Just as Jess was being escorted into her jail cell, the accosted pedestrian, having given her statement to the police, was storming into the boutique where she purchased her purse. She approached the cash and threw the purse at the bewildered owner.

"How can I help you?" asked the owner, averting eye contact.

"It's one of a kind, is it?"

The owner turned a key to open the cash and counted out $200 minus a penny, plus tax.

Jess sat on the concrete floor with her back to the wall, her hair matted, her face bare and colourless.  Mick sat on the floor opposite her, rested his back against the wall and reached through the bars to hold her hand.

"I told you it was stolen, babe."

They slumped down into the fetal position, exhausted, staring into each other's bloodshot eyes.

"Sweet dreams," said Mick.

"Sweet dreams."

MARK HOFFE is a native of St. John's who is pursuing a creative writing career. He won an honorable mention in the 15th Annual Canadian Authors Association Student Writing Contest (1998), and had poems published in "Twig" (1998) and "with an image of grace" (1999), as well as more recent newspaper articles.

# Hunted

## by Heather Lane

There was nothing about the forest glen near Brigus Junction that was out of the ordinary that day. The sky above was littered with clouds that hid the fading sun of the early evening. The leaves in the trees hung from their branches high above, staring down at a figure moving below them.

They seemed to watch as it moved slowly and carefully over the dead fall leaves and litter of the forest floor. To this creature, everything in the forest meant danger. She practically slithered on her belly, trying hard not to make a sound.

Her eyes needed to be everywhere; watching. To be ready to run. To hide. To escape. But in the quiet, the only thing she could hear was her own shallow breath and the gentle, soft sound of rustling leaves beneath her as she moved.

Time seemed to crawl along right beside her. It seemed forever had passed since she had been first followed; hunted as a wild animal. Adrenaline kept her on-edge and jumpy, ready to fuel the muscles she would need to spring and run. She wanted to run now but the risk of getting caught was too great. She needed to stay hidden and keep going.

There was a place ahead, dark and secluded. The hollow log would make a nice place to disappear. She could rest there until danger had past.

She hadn't gotten far when a twig snapped somewhere in the distance.

She froze.

Her breath seemed to catch in her throat. That sound was a lot closer than she expected. Her muscles tensed. She grew nervous. Her eyes darted around looking for the slightest movement. Her stomach twisted in anticipation and she chanced moving more quickly toward her hiding spot when she saw nothing immediately threatening. It had just been a squirrel running through the treetops.

Relaxing a tiny bit, she came to her hands and knees and moved faster. If she could only make it in time. The hole might have been small, but it was big enough for her to crawl into and she turned around, backing into the dark space.

Even the sense of claustrophobia didn't stop her from tucking herself away. With any luck it wouldn't need to be for very long. She tunneled her vision out through the hole to keep watch. She would be safe here.

The ground was cold and damp. She shivered when the chill seemed to creep into her bones. She grew impatient. She longed for freedom. She wanted to be home, safe and sound in a warm bed with a full belly.

Then she heard him.

Right around the corner, the hunter was making his way closer and closer. She froze, drawing her head down lower to the ground. He hadn't noticed her.

Yet.

Her heart pounded.

It was only a matter of time.

He could smell her.

She was around here somewhere. He knew it. His stomach growled at the prospect of lunch and pressed on. If he could catch her, it would be a sweet reward. He could only think of one thing as he listened, sniffed and followed the trail.

He could hear the distant sounds of the birds, a trickling stream and what appeared to be human voices far off somewhere else. They would be no threat to him here. He could continue his hunt undisturbed.

If he listened carefully, she might give herself away. Then it would be all over. He pressed his nose to the ground and sniffed. She had been here but the scent was a little faded. Too cold. Covered with leaves and underbrush, it seemed to get stronger as he moved forward. It grew warmer with each step. His heart lifted. She was here! She was very close, but where?

He shoved his nose under the leaves that scattered the ground and sniffed next to the base of a tree. No, the scent grew cold. His belly rumbled again.

Dinner.

So hungry.

He had to find her.

She trembled and remained still, gulping in anticipation. She sunk deeper into her hole as the tread of his paws on the ground gave his presence away.

She could hear him sniffing her out and she pressed her lips together to mask the sound of her breathing. She panicked. It would be all over soon, she knew it. She needed another place to hide. Somewhere high and out of sight. She was foolish to hide here.

A brief sensation of joy swept through her when she sized up the tree in front of her. Its branches grew low enough for her to climb and would be a perfect escape. He wouldn't be able to get her there. He couldn't climb. She needed a distraction. A ruse to draw his attention.

Picking up a stick that lay on the ground, she threw it into a clump of bushes a few feet away. She heard the whisper of the leaves as it landed in the shrubs and listened as his feet padded eagerly through the brush to the bushes behind her hiding place.

It was now or never.

Wriggling quickly from inside the hollow log, she scrambled to her feet. She was already breathing heavily from holding her breath so much and her lungs strained as she headed for the tree.

It was too late.

"'Lizabet!" A shriek echoed in the glen. "Get in 'ere, my duckie! It's supper time!"

She froze and whirled on the spot as her nan called out to her.

Brandy had spotted her and there was no time to react. She was suddenly bowled over by 60 pounds of fur, teeth and raw canine power when he came hurtling at her from the bushes.

His tail wagged happily as he covered her face with drool and slobber.

Giggling with delight, she tried to get up. But the youthful Labrador had packed on pounds since his puppy days and could easily pin her tiny frame to the ground.

"OK, OK, you found me!" she laughed, and spluttered when she got a mouth full of warm tongue. "Ew!"

"'Lizabet! C'mon honey, 'fore it gets cold!"

Her grandmother peered through the trees as her 12-year-old granddaughter wrestled with the dog.

Elizabeth lifted her head and looked through the trees. "'kay! I'm comin', Nan!"

She got to her feet and patted her leg. Her kissing noise drew him from sniffing out the log where she had been hiding.

"C'mon, Brandy. Dinner time!"

He turned and bounded after her as she walked toward the cabin. He overtook her and galloped inside. There was still only one thought on his mind.

Dinner.

So hungry.

HEATHER LANE was born and raised in St. John's, where she is happily married and the mother of two. She hopes to become an accomplished writer/novelist.

# The Rock

### by Ruby Mann

The feel of the earth beneath my body releases me from the weight of this rock I'm carrying. Tiny pieces of grass and stones are already embedded in my elbows and the strawberries growing in the graveyard are being crushed into my shirt. I notice the ants running over the mounds determinedly, making their way between dandelions and artificial flowers stuck firmly into the ground.

Suddenly, my arms feel weightless, without substance. My heart thumps frighteningly loud in my ears. I think about throwing the rock away before Charles gets here, and my heart slows. I draw comfort from the familiar gravesites, especially my grandmother's.

Lying here in the hot sun, nestling my head on folded arms, I go back over yesterday trying to make sense out of what I saw. I caught them throwing mud at my sister, sitting dangerously close to the edge on a high log over the brook where those wretched boys had put her. As soon as they heard me shout they took off through the trees, but not before I saw his jacket. Or thought I saw it. Everything went fast then, me taking my sister down from the log, my mother asking me what happened, all of it jumbled together. I tell her about the boys but I don't say his name. Even now I don't know why.

That night I prop myself up under the covers with the flashlight, reading "Beverly of Graustark" for the third time, mainly because I love the romantic parts. Charles was the one who gave it to me. "See what you think of this prince," he grinned, knowing full well I was stuck on royalty.

We had finally worked our way out of Nancy Drew and the Hardy Boys and were moving into different books. Our community was too small for a library so we relied on each other for reading material. I hate to admit I am getting hooked on romance, but he isn't one to notice. We don't think of ourselves that way.

To keep myself from crying I light into some vicious swearing, pressing my face into the pillow to keep Mom from hearing. Shit, shit, shit. The ugly words make me feel better.

Shutting off the flashlight I try to sleep, but it's his face I see. I think back over all the times we've had, the picnics at the brook, stealing apples from Mr. Murphy's trees, playing Cops and Robbers, the cricket games in our yard, reading and talking our way through books. I recall how it was when his family was moved from Burin after the tsunami hit.

Now it all feels like history, something done and wrapped up. Mixed in with good memories are the nasty thoughts, rehearsals for the big payback.

I hardly know how I got to the graveyard, waiting for Charles to come, just like he does every other Saturday morning. Nerves are getting the better of me. He calls my name and I stand up, shaky and nervous, not wanting to look at his face as he barrels towards me.

"Hi Maddie, what are we doing?" and I'm struck by how bright everything seems. I know we should talk but I can't stop. He's still smiling when I whack him on the side of the head with all the force of the rock in my hand. Just before he drops to the ground I see the pain on his face, pain mixed with something else.

I start running toward home, breathing hard, feeling the horror of what I've done. I know I should go back, but I can't.

When I get home my mother is there, all normal and casual, as if it were any other day. "Maddie, take the clothes off the line," she says, and now I feel lighter.

I rush around all afternoon looking for jobs, fetching the water for washing and making my mother suspicious. By evening I know for sure it isn't any other day. I play a half-hearted game with my brother, looking constantly over my shoulder, hoping to see *his* face. I welcome the big racket of the supper table in our house and for once I am happy to do my homework without being told.

Still the time drags. The strangeness of Saturday moves into Sunday, a long, hot day with nothing to do but think about him, as the dread of Monday settles into my bones.

I wait at the end of the path for my friend Patricia. She's curious about which book I've borrowed from Charles this time. "Could I read it when you're finished?" she asks.

I have to admit I don't have a new book but she doesn't believe me. She thinks I just won't share, and I let her. Shuffling my way along the road, kicking up dust and stones, I wish I could be in Graustark with Beverly. Real life is nothing like it is in books, I decide. Everything there is neat and tidy and always a happy ending or at least some resolution. I doubt we'll have a happy ending.

I spot him on the playground and for a moment I'm relieved. Maybe it's not going to be so bad. He's laughing with his friends and nothing seems to be awry. Then he sees me and I know that everything has changed. There's an ugly purple bump on the side of his head that I put there.

He says nothing at all to me, not a word. We stand looking at each other across a long distance with the awful knowing that I didn't even give him a chance to explain.

Life returning to normal became a cruel irony for me. I learned there are some distances that can neither be measured nor crossed. We finished high school together but I didn't know how to repair the damage and he didn't seem to care. I went away for university and he left Newfoundland for work.

I was home for a visit when I heard Charles was dying. Seeing him, something familiar settled in my body that time couldn't touch. It had been 15 years since that day in the graveyard and outwardly nothing much had changed. We both looked a little older, but that was all. Yet, I could hardly recognize the distracted man who constantly checked himself in the mirror. I knew he was looking for evidence of what the doctors had told him. Something was eating up his insides. How could he look the same on the outside? That was my question, too.

RUBY MANN lives in Pasadena with her husband, John. She recently studied creative writing at Sir Wilfred Grenfell College in Corner Brook.

# The Flower of Irishville
## by Robert C. Parsons

Sniff, what about the haunt in Skipper Jim's house and the time you were the flower of Irishville?

The haunt, the token. Ah, 'twas a glorious invention and I allow the skipper still thinks about the Saturday nights when he was paid a visit by a token.

Token?

Three Saturday nights last fall I put a ghost by the pantry window in his house. Even if I got to say so myself, 'tis a wonderful haunt, a marvelous idea and I thought of putting it there.

I want to tell Sniff there's no such thing as haunts, and Ma told me, and she says nowadays 'tis only the crowd from the old country who believes in all sorts of fairies and ghosts and little people. But I shut up for fear Sniff will walk out the door with the story he promised not told.

Sniff says, I'll tell you how it come about. In grandmother's sewing basket there's every class of spool of thread you can imagine, number nine, number 10, ought 40, silk thread, cotton, white, black and every colour under the sun, even sky-blue pink.

Sky-blue pink, Sniff?

Oh, ah, 'twas in the stuff left behind by grandmother, God rest her soul, and I got no use for needles and thread and every kind of sewing implement. That's how she kept bread on the table when she was around, everything from knitting cuffs and guernseys to mending sail for the Nellie T. Rixon and many a seaman's clothes bag she stitched up out of an old piece of canvas duck. Even one of merchant Peyton's boss men brought old ripped sailcloth to go over the fish for her to mend. She always said if she got a cent for every button she sewed on…

Never mind. What's sewing thread got to do with the token?

I took a spool of white silk thread and looked at it and you know what was written on the little label, just what yer eyes could pick out? It was tiny writing that said, "A hundred yards of thread on a spool."

A hundred yards, how much, how far is that, Sniff?

Exactly my question. Exactly. How far could it go? And I thought it might go right over a house, and 'twas at that very minute Sniff's Haunting Scheme was born. After supper, I picked the biggest house around to test out an amazing way to conjure up an apparition.

I want to ask Sniff about the big words he's using and could he speak in plain English, but before I got it out he says, Made a loop, put it around my wrist so I could hold on to one end, and I pitched the spool over Skipper Jim's house, and pitched the spool as high as I could, and it went over the house and landed on the other side.

And what's that got to do with a ghost and a token?

Well, I fetched a four inch nail and tied it to the end of the thread and pulled it up abreast of the back pantry window and the nail went click, click, click, against the window. Now, I'm on the other side of the house in the bush, pulling on the thread, a silk thread like catgut, strong enough it would never burst. It was a fantastic scheme and one that was never thought of before in Irishville, and perhaps nowhere else in the world.

I say to Sniff: The click, click, click?

Yes, the nail when I pulled on the thread from way over would touch the window and tap, tap. When the light came on in the pantry, I pulled on the thread a little and the nail tapped against the glass. Click, click, tap, tap. Only when Skipper's missus looked out the window to see what it was I stopped and pulled up the nail up past the window so she wouldn't see it.

'Twas a ghost, or what you call it, a token, to them.

Ah, half-hour later, I pulled on it again until someone came to the pantry window and looked out, looked all around. Two of them even came outside with a flashlight, but I pulled the nail up past the window and they couldn't see it and they couldn't see me. Perhaps they looked for a twig scraping or a loose shingle or something, but 'twas nothing to be seen, nobody around and no footprints or anything in the mud under the window. I left it in place and every Saturday night for three Saturdays in a row I pulled on the thread. That's why I call it Sniff's Haunting Scheme, and what a marvelous idea, even if I say so myself.

God help you, Sniff, and I hope He will. What if?

The questions, the questions, and God helps the ones who help themselves. I would have kept it there but a storm of wind blew the No. 10 thread and four-inch nail away. Ah, the skipper often speaks of tokens of dead seamen. Spirits could come back and tap on the window at night and if they were drowned on a Saturday night, then they'd come back and go click, click, click on the window every Saturday night.

Ah, yes, a token.

Skipper Jim looked out the window them Saturday nights and envisioned something, perhaps a token, a symbol, you know, a sign of a lost soul. But I allow he had a suspicion and I think he knew somebody, a human being, was behind it all.

He thought 'twas you, Sniff?

Ah, yes. He met me afterwards when I was standing on the road and looking up at his big house and I think he had a suspicion then, an idea 'twas something that walked on two legs was the haunt. T'were no token.

And that's when he called you the idjet.

"Idiot," the skipper says, "a blooming idiot."

Ah, Sniff. Ah, and you said, "Yes sir, the flower of Irishville."

ROBERT C. PARSONS was born and lives in Grand Bank. Married with three children, he was an educator for 30 years and is the author of several books about ships, sailors and the sea, including "Wind and Wave," "Between Sea and Sky," and "Saltwater Tales," volumes I and II.

# How Far is Nowhere?

## by Chad Pelley

The clouds, rendered pink by the setting sun, looked like cotton candy. They hung so low in the sky that Martin felt like a giant, like he could reach out and bite them, chew them, taste them. He sank a hand into the pocket of his faded-to-white jeans — freckled red with fish guts and worm viscera — and hauled out his Player's Light regulars. The pocket was so deep and tight he had to wrestle his hand back out. Out of habit, he licked his dry and flaky lips before placing the cigarette between them. Flakes of skin had always sat on his lips like snowflakes. Whenever he drifted off into one of his melancholic daydreams, he'd chew at those flakes.

He sat on the edge of his father's old fish stage, staring out at the sea that had swallowed him whole nine years ago. *Too old to be at it, too stubborn to admit it.* The sea spat his father out in Tors Cove, under the dilapidated wharf, three weeks after he'd gone missing. They could only assume it was him. The pattern on his red and black plaid shirt still looked about right, and there was no talk around the coast of any other fishermen having gone missing that month.

Martin stared at the water now, wondering how it had conducted his father's body. He imagined the dense, salty water holding his father like a puppet, steering his limbs slowly and independently in different directions. Maybe like some kind of poetic dance. Maybe it was a peaceful departure. He left out the images of a body thrust onto jagged rocks. Each blow like a shark bite. He left out the sensation of his father's lungs and guts filling with water until they popped like a balloon. An itch at his ankle tore him out of his daze. A fly bite. But his knee-high rubber boots were suctioned too tightly around his shins for him to slide his hand down. He could only punch at his ankle to numb the itch. He hated mosquitoes, and carried a pocket-sized bottle of Deep Woods insect repellent at all times. Even in the winter, it was in his jacket pocket. Sometimes it leaked and made a soup of his keys and coins.

He clicked his Zippo open and shut a few times before lighting the cigarette. He liked the sound it made, he liked the act of preparing for the cigarette more than he liked smoking it: pausing his day, sitting down, clinking his bronze Zippo open and shut, and taking his world in. He'd won the lighter, along with Burt Caine's last $20, in a game of 120s down in Aquaforte years ago. Back when they still fished in his community, back before his brother moved up to Alberta, before his father died, before his mother left his father to find a man who could be more available to her, and before her sister married the haughty accountant she'd met at Memorial University. He clicked it open one last time, flicked the wheel, so dry and corroded that it tore at his flesh — a friction burn — and breathed the flame in through his cigarette.

The wind was vicious, and the smoke left the red tip like a string held loosely in the air by invisible hands. He watched three squawking gulls hang in the sky, moving only up and down, not right to left, waiting for a break in the wind. It howled like the devil's choir. The water, infinitely rippled by it, looked like meringue on account of all the white crests. The howling of the wind was the only sound Martin heard these last few months, and he was sick of its gnawing, melancholic weeping. When the wind did die down in the mornings, the only other sound was the constant gush of water off land, like footsteps across a stony beach. He vowed to be the last man to leave the forsaken place, and now, when he left, he would be. He considered himself the captain of a ship, obliged to drown with her, or at least be the last man off. It gave some vague sense of purpose to his unwillingness to pack up and leave like all the others had.

There were no fish left in the sea he sat staring at, and what was there, wasn't his to take. Not anymore. Everyone else could move on, as people had been doing for almost two decades now, as if their sense of self and culture was that malleable. As if rebirth was that simple. It wasn't a refusal to change that prevented Martin from living another life; it was an *inability* to change. His community had fled up North or over to Alberta in three big droves, except the Noseworthy clan — they all set up shop in Carbonear, and some of the younger ones took up university or college in St. John's and Stephenville. All of the trades were out for Martin though. His fingers rose up from his hand like thick, crooked twigs — horribly disfigured from poorly healed broken bones. They were chipped and dinged and scarred pink by feisty crabs, stray fish hooks and hundred-pound barrels or boats dropped onto his hand. The last three fingers of his left hand were functionally useless. Frostbite. From the night he and his brother had gone looking for their father.

Martin's lungs filled with a sharp pain now, and still stung long after he'd blown the grey smoke back out. Spaced-out and staring at the sea, he'd smoked the cigarette down past the filter, the cherry almost touching his yellowed fingers. He flicked the butt away, disgusted, and watched the wind carry it down to his father's old wharf. The butt stumbled along the tree trunks the wharf was built of, until it settled into a groove between two trunks, next to a distinctive splotch of white. The place was only a dumping ground for gulls now. Gulls that had long ago stopped searching his boat and stage for remnants of fish. The wharf ran up from the sea to his father's old stage like a rug. Decades of gutting and storing fish had once stained its floor a crimson red, and filled it with a palpable stench of cod. Now the wind and rain had wiped it clean, as sterile as an operating room.

His baby blue dory was knocking off the wharf now that the wind had changed. Persistently. As if calling out to him, as if it was cold and lonely and bored. The red trim that once encircled the top few inches of his boat was more flaked off than left on.

He certainly wasn't going to go back to university at 43, to be gawked at by smug city kids, as if he were some cliché relict that the "new" Newfoundland was embarrassed of. His mind wasn't for that anyway, even if there was anything taught there that he could try to wrap his mind around. He stuck another cigarette between his dry, chapped lips and clicked his Zippo open and shut. Open. Shut. Open. Flick. He rose with the smoke of his first inhale. He had to silence the boat. He walked past a crow searching through the stones on the beach. It had only to spread its wings, and the wind scooped it up.

Night had crept in quickly and sucked the red out of the sky. The clouds looked black, not white, against the midnight blue all around him. He untied the frayed, yellow rope connecting his boat to the wharf. There was an art to how he worked with his fingers, compensating for how each was incompetent on its own. They had to work synergistically or not at all, like a team of rowers. He held the rope like a leash now, peering down at the boat. It looked like a dog who wanted a walk. It wanted to be out on the sea.

Something beyond him had made the decision for him, as if strings had fallen from the sky above and made a marionette of him. He climbed into his boat and lay in it like a cot, using his flannel jacket as a pillow. He was done thinking now. The rest was up to the sea. Within minutes, the coastline looked as far away as England. The land looked inches high. Only the clinking of his Zippo interrupted the lulling sound of the water. Even the birds weren't out that far.

# The Dixie Challenger

## by Benedict Pittman

My collection of dinkies in the summer of 1982 was impressive, but my cars from television and cinema were most sought after. The Dixie Challenger was my pride and joy, not the actual General Lee from "The Dukes of Hazzard" but a close knock-off – orange, with mag wheels and a Dixie flag decal.

My family was new to Stephenville and I hadn't yet made any friends, so I grabbed my pillowcase of dinkies and travelled alone to the dirt pile. One of the local kids had the same admiration for my particular gutter because he was already up to his eyeballs in dust and dinkies. I dumped my payload and he fixated on them until I asked, "Can I play?" He immediately agreed, said his name was Stan and we spent hours racing our cars through roads grooved with a Popsicle stick.

Donny appeared. He was taller and more solid than my scrawny body. He approached us with folded arms. "This is my spot. My house is right there." He pointed to one apartment in an eight-plex. Stan was accustomed to this process and swiftly handed Donny his favourite, the "Smokey and the Bandit" Trans Am. "Give him your best one," Stan whispered. I scrambled through my cars and found a good one, not my best. I handed him a red semi that resembled the one from "B.J. and the Bear." He reluctantly agreed and we played. There were 10-car pile-ups on the freeway, demolition derbies and even a funeral procession. At dusk I said goodbye to my new friends, Stan ran home and Donny helped me collect my cars.

"You comin' down tomorrow?"

"Sure!"

I had a friend!

Donny leered at me, "I like the rig, but it's not your best dinky." I wondered if he had seen my Dixie Challenger.

I met Donny at the dirt pile the next day. He had urgent news: "Stan got your 'Chips' motorbikes!" I searched the dinky bag and sure enough, the bikes were missing. Donny led me to the playground. Stan was carving his name into a swing and Donny, with uncanny speed, pinned him to the ground. "Give him back the 'Chips' bikes!"

"I don't have them!" squealed Stan as Donny's knees compressed his chest. He asked repeatedly, but Stan denied the theft. Donny leaned over Stan's face, "Here comes the rain, Stan." Donny cleared his throat, hawked up a mass of spit and released it over Stan's crying eyes – the thing was still connected to his mouth. Donny sucked it back up. "I guess a bigger blob then!"

Stan dug into his pockets, dropped the 'Chips' bikes and raced home.

"I told you," he bragged as he returned the bikes. "I get to pick the best dinky, for real this time and it's mine ... for good." I tried to argue but Donny was adamant, snatching the bag and peering inside. He took the Dixie Challenger.

Time slowed.

I said nothing, did nothing but watch my favourite dinky sink into Donny's tight pockets.

"I'm having a sleepover tomorrow. Come over after supper."

I nodded, unsure of what happened. Donny went home and I sat on the swing. My favourite dinky, it rolled beautifully and jacked up like a monster truck. Could I buy another? No ... Matchbox had stopped making them. Donny had helped get the bikes back, but at what price? It wasn't a fair exchange; I would give half my dinkies for the Dixie Challenger.

The sleepover was as I expected, except for Stan's presence. Why he would be there after such a humiliating experience is anyone's guess, but Donny was the king. Our host's mother made us hot-dogs and seven pre-pubescent boys spilled mustard as they watched 'Solid Gold,' the perfect time to search for the Challenger.

While Donny directed our eyes to his favourite dancer, I excused myself to go to the bathroom. I didn't have to search long — the car was sitting on Donny's dresser between his home-run trophies. I pilfered my prized dinky, returned to the gold satin suits of those toned beauties and tried to forget about it.

The next day, I returned to the dirt pile, minus my favourite. I laid my bag to the side and began to make the first road.

"I didn't take it! Please Donny!" shrieked a terrified Stan. I raced behind Donny's place to investigate. He had Stan on the ground next to his dog's house. The glob of spit drifted in the wind, still connected to Donny's bottom lip and inches from Stan's cheek.

"I was good enough to let you come to my sleepover and you took my dinky!"

Stan denied his accused sin as Donny sucked up the glob and pushed Stan's face closer to a doggy dropping. Then he spotted me, "Get over here!"

I stood over Stan as Donny commanded me, "Hawk a good one."

"I can't ... he didn't ... how do you know he took the dinky?" I frantically played dumb.

Donny barked, as did his dog. "Spit!"

I straddled Stan's head and proceeded to rip my throat out from coughing up a sizeable glob of multi-coloured saliva. I let it drop, but it was too heavy, I couldn't suck it back up! The thing splattered across Stan's face. He went still, just staring at me. Then he began to shake and growl. Donny rode a bucking bronco. Stan jolted like he was having a fit but Donny was simply too heavy for him. He frothed at the mouth and screamed a multitude of curses, directing his rage at me.

Donny looked up at me: "I know it was you."

How could he know? "What? I didn't take anything."

Donny stared through me. He knew. "You stole it from my room!" He was certain.

"No," I lied.

"No one else would dare," he proclaimed. "Stan, you want to kill him?" Stan fumed and shook. Donny narrowed his gaze, "Get him!" He released the beast and I ran.

Stan's fury was at my heels as Donny's laughter trailed behind. I snatched my bag as Stan reached for any part of me. Somehow, I managed to get to my house. I peeked out the window as Stan paced. After a few minutes, Donny joined him. "We'll get you tomorrow!"

I grew pale as the summer waned. Halfway through my third week of exile, there was a knock. Donny was on the front step. I went to the window but did not open the door.

"We're playin' spotlight!"

I was suspicious. "What about the dinky?"

"What? Oh … that. I forgot all about it. Come on, there's girls playing!"

"You're not mad?" I opened the door.

"I was just having fun. Here …" He handed me a couple of my Hot Wheels dragsters. "They musta got mixed up with mine. You comin'?"

I hauled on my Velcro Sprinters, but hesitated. Was this a trick? Dozens of kids around for spotlight and he wants me? Would I owe a favour to Donny Corleone? I slowly walked out of my prison and smelled the fresh-cut grass. There had to be conditions to my release. It couldn't be this easy.

He stopped me on the front lawn. "Uh … you got a flashlight?"

BENEDICT PITTMAN is a writer, director and actor. Originally from Stephenville, he now lives in St. John's. His works have been supported by the Canada Council for the Arts and the Newfoundland and Labrador Arts Council. In 2005, Ben won the Arts and Letters Award for Dramatic Script for his play "The Privateer," and again in 2008 for his play "The Fights."

# The Inheritance

## by Martin Poole

Jordan thought the Trinity Bay coastline looked like a sprawled hand and the houses nestled there like sprinkles of coarse salt. There's Port Union, he thought, the place where I was born. He brought his camera to his eyes as Glenn caught up to him, gasping for air. Glenn stood beside him at the cliffside, bracing the bottom of his fly rod against the mossy ground, and followed his gaze.

"That's Port Union straight ahead … and where the quay leads is Catalina," Glenn said.

"So that's Port Union," Jordan said, taking his ball cap off to part his brown hair away from his eyes. "You never get a view like this in St. John's."

Glenn straightened his back, holding his head higher. "No sir. And that you don't."

"Why do you stay here? There can't be much to do."

He looked at Glenn's thatched mustache which covered his mouth, his weak chin which jutted beneath, and his broad hands which were scarred and calloused from labour. The wind gusted, blowing his faded blue jeans taut, exposing his thin legs which led to his white sneakers, soiled and ripped at the edges. "I'm sorry if that sounded —"

"No … no," Glenn said, "I never thought about it, that's all. There isn't much to do, but the people are good. You get used to it."

Jordan turned to the view.

"How's your mother?" Glenn asked.

"Good. She's going back to school soon. Besides that she's busy with stuff around the house."

"It's good she's keeping busy," Glenn said. "She married?"

Jordan looked at him timidly, like a child caught in a lie. "Yeah, she is."

Glenn sighed, "Laura always wanted to get married."

A cumulous cloud sauntered overhead, casting a heavy shadow that cooled their perspiration. Jordan took off his sunglasses and polished the dusty lenses with his shirt. Glenn eyed Jordan's face delicately.

"Is he a good man?"

Jordan put on his sunglasses and his foot started to scuff gravel into narrow mounds like river ripples. He looked at Glenn, meeting his identical eyes. Jordan's foot stopped.

"Yeah, he's OK. Mom is really happy."

Jordan pressed his foot into the ripples, leaving his footprint.

Glenn looked at it ponderously. "She was right to leave here."

"But why did you stay?"

"I don't know. I guess I felt I could make a good life for us here by fishing."

The wind held, as if the sky had exhaled enough and was now drawing a deep breath. Silence makes silence louder, thought Jordan. How can anyone live here? He turned to the remaining trail, and they both walked towards it with their faces forward, passive to each other and their surroundings. The trail led them downhill into a valley which stopped the wind completely, leaving Jordan to combat the flies by slapping his bare forearms.

"They're attracted to bright colours, you know," Glenn said, looking at Jordan's bright yellow T-shirt which cast gold hues over his face.

Jordan looked down at his sandals, then at his khaki cargo shorts. "I guess I'm not dressed for this."

The trail began to taper like a steeple, so they walked single file with their arms closely cradled by the trees. Then the trees parted and Jordan could see a fork in the trail ahead.

"The pond is to the left," his father said behind him, then added, "Barrett's Pond."

"Where does this lead?" Jordan asked, pointing to the other side.

"To the Break."

"The break?"

"It's an old dam that fell."

"How did it fall?"

"They say the design was faulty. Laura and I thought it was thunder until we heard the water come down." He wheezed, and coughed. "It came down so hard the ground shook."

Close to the fork, Jordan could see the weed-ridden trail to the Break and the path to Barrett's Pond, with its surface worn brick-hard. "I'd like to see it," he said.

Glenn's face held, and Jordan saw something in it that brought to life a memory of Glenn building a shed, while he held nails in an old peanut can. Another glimpse came then of hitting waves on a dory and feeling the salty spray on his face while Glenn steered with one hand, the other clasped tightly on his shoulder. But it was roots that led nowhere, plot-less dust recollections. Jordan wondered if his decision to meet his father came too late, and if it was better left as is.

"We can go there for a minute. Soon it'll be too late for the trout, you know."

They walked at the river's edge, pausing momentarily as Glenn flicked his fly rod like a whip, causing the fly to dance on the ripples. His movements were deft and calculated, but found nothing. They walked farther, coming to a pond with a barrier at the front. The barrier, where intact, was crawling with vines, its cracks jammed with long yellow grass and serrated weeds. The river flowed powerfully through the middle, pounding the rocks below with a shaking force. The rail that lined the dam was now bent down into the river, twisted over itself, as if it had attempted to escape the catastrophe and slither into the trees. Standing above everything was a metal pole painted black, with a wheel crank that stared endlessly at its own ruin.

Jordan's father stepped ahead, his eyes gaping. "Me and Laura would come here all the time. It was beautiful back then."

Jordan looked, pulled out his digital camera and aimed it towards the twisted rail. He came closer to the waterfall, its din thrumming in his ears, overthrowing all other sound. His father continued, the edges of his eyes glinting.

"She would lean against that rail and watch the kids swim. You were only a bulge in her belly then."

Jordan steadied himself at the edge of the Break.

Glenn looked at his reflection in the water. "I was scared, Jordan. I stayed because I was scared to —"

The camera flash flared like false lightning, and his father blinked. Jordan walked back up the barrier with his eardrums still resonating.

"Perfect," Jordan said, "if only the flies would keep away."

MARTIN POOLE was born and raised in Newfoundland outports but lives in St. John's. He's dabbled in visual arts and music for much of his life but now enjoys writing as therapy between his jobs.

# The Passing

## by Marilyn Pumphrey

She lay on the hospital bed, dying.

A palliative care nurse approached her bed as though it were a sacrificial altar. And every question was capped with "Dear." Elaine felt like saying, "I'm not your 'dear.' Get lost." But she couldn't speak. She needed her breath to request medication when pain gnawed at her innards.

They kept asking her to eat, seeming not to know that she was past food. They kept swabbing inside her fetid mouth with glycerin sticks, the cotton tip gliding over her bare front gums where her partial plate should be. She looked like hell without her teeth. Where did false teeth go when their owner croaked?

"Would you like me to plump up your pillow, dear?" Elaine dragged her eyes open. The nurse with the black roots in her hair was smiling serenely. Teddy bears in blue and pink rompers tumbled across the white background of her smock. Kim scooped a multi-ringed hand under Elaine's head, prying out the pillow with her other hand.

"Christ." Elaine opened her eyes. Every movement was torture to her decimated body. But the nurse was determined to make her comfortable, even if it killed her. That was funny — being killed in the Palliative Care Unit.

"There. Is that better, dear?" Kim beamed.

She was so tired of it. Tired of the oxygen that no longer helped; the whispered conversations, the consoling pats, the sad looks and awkward goodbyes. She knew the palliative care philosophy — to make you comfortable and keep you pain-free while you passed away ... or on ... or over. In fact, while you just plain "passed." This was becoming a new term for dying. Pardon me while I pass.

She remembered joking months ago with her cousin about how she'd like to die. "I don't want to have a heart attack" (she pounded on her left breast) "or a stroke" (she put her head on the side and let her tongue loll). "I'd like a nice little cancer to give me enough time to make my will and make my soul." She'd laughed then, but it no longer seemed amusing.

Then she realized that the pain had returned to the old familiar spot in her left lung. She knew that when night came the cancer took over, eating her body. She'd told Mark that each little cancer cell nudged the others, saying "C'mon boys, she's asleep. Let's nail the liver tonight."

"Elaine." She recognized the voice of her cousin, Marlene, one of "the watchers." Every bed in the unit was ringed with watchers of various sizes and degrees of closeness to the patient. You could tell their rank by their expressions: spouses choked back tears, sisters-in-law daubed occasionally, and cousins looked sad and sniffed. Marlene had broken rank and become a dauber.

Why didn't they leave her alone? If she had the strength, she'd tell them to get out of her face, out of her room. At first, she'd been afraid that she'd die alone, but now she didn't care. They couldn't go with her. They could only be there when she left — like seeing someone off at the airport.

The pain was changing now, sharpening. She felt her heart hammering against her ribs. It was stressed. Would her heart stop beating and her brain realize she was dead an instant before her body shut down? Frightened, she opened her eyes again. The watchers were all down at the end of the bed, turned towards the TV and talking about some stupid movie. Didn't they know that she was the prime-time feature tonight?

The gnawing in her left side was vicious. She needed their attention to get some help. Sucking in her breath, she moaned, simultaneously trying to move her left arm. It worked. Marlene's eyes locked with hers and she touched Mark's sleeve. He turned, walking quickly to the bed.

"What time's her next injection?" demanded Marlene.

"Not for half an hour." He looked at the waterproof watch Elaine had given him for Christmas.

"Ring the buzzer."

Mark hesitated.

"Go on, she needs it," Marlene's voice had an edge. "It's not like she's going to get addicted at this stage of the game."

Elaine moaned again, hating them all. After eons of pain, Kim loomed cheerfully at her bedside, needle in hand.

"We'll fix you up in no time, dear." Untying the neckline of her mauve nightdress, the nurse opened the butterfly shunt and shot the morphine cocktail into the small tube that went directly into Elaine's vein. Gradually, it began to wash through her system.

"She'll rest now, poor darling."

But rest wasn't on the agenda that night. Although a warm drowsiness enfolded her, it had a different quality from her usual torpor. If Elaine didn't know better, she'd swear she was being warmed by the summer sun. A sound of water rattling through stones made her open her eyes.

"Holy shit! Deer Park!"

She was sitting beside a clump of alder bushes on her favourite rock, fishing line dangling into the shining depths. This quiet pool was the best corner of her best trout stream, and here she was, rubber boots and all.

"Getting any bites?"

The voice behind her was familiar and she turned sharply. There was no mistaking the baseball cap jammed down backwards over the dark curls. "Bud. What the hell are you doing here?"

"Well, I ain't laying a carpet." The blue eyes were as mischievous as ever. He moved his sneakered foot, giving his fishing basket a prod.

"But you can't be fishing. You're friggin' dead."

"That's a dirty word over here."

"Here where?"

She looked around. "Aren't we in Deer Park?"

"Of course we are, Old Trout." He put a warm hand on her shoulder and gestured to a gravel lane behind them. "And right down the road's me cabin, with Cec and Nell stokin' up the barbie."

"This is a dream, right?"

But looked at her intently. Then he slapped at a mosquito buzzing past his face. "Damn flies would drive you cracked."

"What's going on?"

"Listen to me. I've got a six-pack of Blue just waitin' to slide down your throat. Are you comin'?" Picking up his fishing basket, he turned towards the lane.

Elaine hesitated. She knew there was something she had to do.

"Where's Mark?"

"He's not here ... C'mon, the beers getting warm," said Bud, starting up the path.

She sat motionless. "I can't go yet." Elaine rose and hovered at the edge of the water, then, taking a step onto an unsteady rock, she almost toppled headfirst.

"Christ!"

"Let me help you." She took Bud's strong hand, and the scene shifted, like a turned card in a game of Growl. Suddenly, she was back in the misery of her hospital bed, and the hand she was holding was Mark's familiar one.

"It's OK to go."

She dredged up the words she'd neglected saying during the last weeks of her illness when her wasted body was the centre of her universe: his constant care, unnoticed.

"Love you … thanks … goodbye."

Then she was back in Deer Park with the sun on her face and Bud's hand in hers, warm and steady.

"You all right?"

"I'm friggin' fantastic. Let's go for the Blue."

MARILYN PUMPHREY, a native of St. John's, has written plays for radio and the stage. She has worked as a freelancer and reporter for newspapers, and written magazine articles and a who's who of women in Newfoundland and Labrador. She is the author of "Littleseal — The Life and Adventures of a Harp Seal Pup."

# Uncle Ned's Turnips
## by Jaime Pynn George

No matter how bad things got here in Harbour Grace, business was always good for Mr. Willis Mortimer Martin. When times were rough, as they often were, he was always on top of things.

He owned a little vegetable farm up on the hill and no matter how poorly everyone else's crops were doing, his were always big and bright and plentiful. He was a well-respected gent with a blissful disposition, warm eyes and a real knack for dressing sharply.

I looked up to that man from the time I was a tot, so you can imagine how I felt when he asked me to run the vegetable stand one summer when I was about 14. That particular year was a bad one and nothing grew for anyone, that is except for Mr. Martin. The crops from Martin's fields were lush and juicy and perfect in every way. The carrots and turnips were especially brilliant — so sweet you could draw nourishment from a mere whiff of their clean, crisp flesh.

Money was as sparse as food at the time, but that was of no odds to Mr. Martin. Everyone needed to put food on the table, so as generous as he was admired, Mr. Martin let no one go unfed.

He didn't only draw money from the one venture. Old Willis was also a merchant and caretaker for the local cemetery. The taking of me under his wing meant that I would never have to worry much about running out of work and ensured me future success. I was sorely indebted to that man in a very short time.

Every duty I performed for Mr. Martin brought me great pleasure, except when he called upon me to check on the cemetery from time to time. There weren't any streetlights like there are today, and folks at the time liked to regale each other with stories about just how haunted the old place was.

It was a peculiar ominous garden of moss. It didn't matter how clear the night; there was always a shroud of hanging fog lurking suspiciously inside the hallowed gates. Proper markers were strewn as if without much thought amongst hosts of homemade wooden crosses and boulders, one last prayer for immortality. I always heard some whisper, saw some vapour to unnerve me.

One cool dusky night, in particular, was to bring my work for Willis Martin to an end, and scarcely a day goes by when I don't relive those cold and dizzy moments.

Mr. Martin did nothing to quiet the rumours about the old burial yard. In fact, he was very much an instigator and could be found many a night at the local pub spinning tales of ghosts and the misfortune of curious youth at the gates of the hilltop graveyard. His yarns were what unnerved me most; knowing that he had come from a long line of gravediggers, it was hard not to take his gruesome accounts as gospel.

The old man asked me to meet him alone and with great secrecy at 10 o'clock sharp in back of the cemetery. I obliged, half-heartedly.

There he stood, in his best dressed, shovel in hand next to what appeared to be an open grave. My senses had not deceived me, it was indeed an open grave; one of Ms. Ethel Mary Sheppard. I swayed in a stupor of disbelief and wonder. The stench was unnerving, thick like rotted cabbage.

Her blue dress, I still remember, looked wet and clotted after a mere couple of weeks beneath the dirt. I know I must have screamed. Everything blurred as I heard his steady voice. "Get to digging her up, b'y, we don't have all night!"

I cannot say if I spoke a word through the clot of horror that nested at the back of my throat. I remember my sway worsening as I tried to blink the blur of tears from my eyes.

"Don't go being foolish, b'y. Old Ethel never hurt no one living, she sure ain't gonna hurt you dead! She was a good church-going woman and she would be proud to know she was doing some good."

Looking around in the moonlight, everything became nauseatingly clear. I noticed as if for the first time the flowers and trees growing on each grave amongst the mossy earth. It seemed as though there was a powerful fertilizer nourishing the ground from within.

"She'll bring some mighty fat carrots, my boy. Remember them big potatoes we had last year? They were Annie Burden's. There's no fertilizer in the world so good as the blessed, and these here were blessed by Father Patrick himself. And I tell you we've had some fine turnips," he said, waving his hand to one far-off, moss-encased stone, "but none so big as we got from poor old Uncle Ned."

JAIME PYNN GEORGE is a graduate of Memorial University and a fan of horror stories and "strange but true" tales who lives in Harbour Grace.

# The Boom Run

## by Peter Daniel Shea

He stopped for the third time, slightly stooped, one hand on his hip, the other on his cane. He looked at the gravel before him on the road. Closing his eyes, he remembered walking briskly up this hill, his kit on his back, his rifle over his shoulder, the fresh air filling his lungs. The destination was all that mattered then, the seeking of it. Now with every step there was attention, effort, focus.

His grandson touched his arm. We're almost there, there's no rush. Take your time. He looked back over his shoulder at the broad vista of Freshwater Bay, the town of Gambo tucked in under the ridge, the white spruce soaring into the sunlight. The highway had cut a swath through the forest along the ridge, but the view had not changed. The blue reach of the bay, the pacing estuary, the meandering rocky river and the broad marsh that framed it to the south. It was the same as he remembered from long, long ago.

There were submarines in the bays then, they said. The long reach of Bonavista Bay ended at Gambo, and the airbase at Gander was no more than 10 miles away as the crow flew. The Germans were anything if not resourceful.

The Cape Breton Highlanders came to St. John's by ship from Halifax. Fresh-faced and handsome in their kilts and tams, he and his mates stepped off at the train station in Gambo, and moved into a newly built barracks on the northern ridge. They established themselves, a squad at the train station, a post high on the ridge, and they patrolled the path down along the bay into Dark Cove and Middle Brook.

The town had grown up narrowly along the river, a channel for spruce logs that were corralled and shipped by train to the pulp mill at Grand Falls. The families of the town, many of whom had sons overseas in the Royal Navy or in the Forestry Service in Scotland, treated the boys from Cape Breton as their own. It was the spring of 1942.

He first saw Margaret while on patrol. Her home was near the road, and she was in the front garden, picking black currants from a bush near the porch. He wished her a good morning as he passed by, and she waved a return, her blue eyes sparkling as she smiled.

They danced at the parish hall on Saturday evenings. One night, they walked along the railbed in the moonlight, the air heavy with lilac from the Morrissey's garden. They held each other, and he remembered the warmth of her, the smell of lavender in her hair. He twisted with shock as a shot was fired from the train station near the dock, and ran hand in hand with Margaret back to the parish hall. As he sprinted to the dock, he saw two of his mates frantically trying to start the generator that powered the search light. Looking out beyond the dock to the blackness of the river, he saw a long, low outline, trailing a wake. He froze, and in that moment of indecision the generator roared to life, the searchlight sweeping the reach. The beam played over a massive boom log that was clipping along with the ebb of the river, trailing branches in its wake. A week of heavy rain had floated the log from where it had beached upriver in the boom run. The tension passed, and someone in the hastily gathered squadron laughed with relief. He laughed as well, the sweat through his shirt and soaking his hair.

Soon it was 1944, and the Allies had crossed the channel. No one talked anymore of submarines in the bays. His regiment was shipping back to Halifax for transport to England and on to Italy. I will come back for you Margaret, he said.

He wrote Margaret from the plaza in Orvieto, in the dust and the sun, smoking a cigarette an American soldier had given him. They were pushing the Germans back over the Alps. I will see you soon, he wrote.

While heading back to the front near Parma, he saw his brother Cameron as the lorry carrying his squadron to the rear for leave passed his own. He called and waved to Cameron, and silently gave thanks that his brother was alive to go home to his parents in Ingonish. Later that day, as his regiment was massing for a push near the Taro River, the news reached him that Cameron had been killed. A stray artillery shell had struck his lorry, killing all aboard. He saw Cameron waving, framed in the sunlight, and a numbness spread through him like ice.

They were pinned down on the banks of the Taro River, the Germans on the high ground on the opposing bank, and the raging water between them. A brief discussion with his captain, and after dark he entered the river where its current was strongest, and swam with a cool ferocity to the other bank. A grenade in the machine-gun nest, a red-flare to his mates, and the crossing was theirs. The regimental commander pinned the medal of valour to his chest later that month at Piacenza.

A letter to his mother, and the long journey home. His father, with tears in his eyes, shook his hand at the train station. His mother was at the window in the kitchen as he came through the door. She looked to him, and without a word looked to the window again.

You have mail from Newfoundland, his father said. He opened the letter from Margaret's sister Teresa, dated some three months previous. Margaret had caught scarlet fever during the winter and died. She was 19.

He sat with his children and grandchildren at his home on Vancouver Island on New Year's Day, discussing their plans for the coming year. His wife had died four years ago, and he had not travelled off the island in years. I want to go to Newfoundland he said, the sudden declaration drawing surprised looks from his children. I served there during the war he said, and I've never been back. His children nodded. In the past, when pressed, he had told them stories of his postings in England and Italy. He had never mentioned Newfoundland.

He and his grandson crested the steep road to the graveyard. The quiet was broken only by the songbirds in the surrounding forest. They had driven through the town earlier in the day. The barracks, school, parish hall, train station and hotel were all gone. All that remained of Margaret's house was a field of wild flowers and nettles, a black currant bush near the new road. There were no logs in the river, no children anywhere to be seen.

He found her, Margaret Mary White, born January 15, 1926, died February 27$^{th}$, 1945. He rested his gnarled hand on the cool stone and closed his eyes. The breeze through the lilac trees just beyond the fence brushed his face. Did you know her, his grandson asked. I did, he answered. I did.

PETER DANIEL SHEA was born and raised in Gander. He's lived and worked in St. John's since 1995 and now lives near Bowring Park with his spouse, Cathy Hoyles, and daughter, Nell.

# Buried Treasure

## by Tina Mardel Stewart

Kate and I had already been given Uncle Charlie's "Tools can be dangerous" lecture, after which, being 10 and 12 respectively, we exchanged little know-it-all smiles. It was another day helping him in the boathouse. While Uncle Charlie, who never had kids with Aunt Ruth, puttered around us, we sat in puddles of sun that pushed through grime on the windows as we worried a waterlogged plank in the floor of the ancient shed.

Our summer visits at the edge of Conception Bay were such fun. Aunt Ruth said we brought laughter to life and Uncle Charlie called us "The Girls." That's how his e-mails came to us — Subject line: To The Girls from UC. Kate and I always rushed to read them knowing he sent stories about neat discoveries along the shore.

So, there we were, that day, helping to pull up black soggy boards from under crusty old nails so Uncle Charlie could keep his grand-dad's boathouse alive. We were in no hurry to finish the job; a little bit of wood breaking loose and crumbling into the pile beside us was enough. Kate was always coming up with "What ifs" and, of course, I would add my two cents' worth.

"What if, years ago, there were pirates on this shore?" Kate sighed as she levered up another sliver of salted wood.

"I'll bet there were and, you know what, maybe Uncle Charlie's grand-dad saw them. I don't think that'd be weird, do you?" I smiled as my piece of wood gave way.

When she concentrated on a tough bit near the old nail, Kate's tongue stuck out. Mom used to say Kate's habit was like Michael Jordan's when he was driving to the basket for another slam-dunk. As Kate's older sister, I thought her habit was kind of cute — for a 10-year-old.

The breeze through the boathouse doorway was cool but puddles of sunshine and our efforts made us hot. Uncle Charlie came over to help pry the stubborn crusty nail and I guess he was ready for a break because he suggested we stop for a snack. At the same time, we heard voices coming down from the house and Aunt Ruth call, "It's snack time." She and Uncle Charlie had been together for so long, they must have known what each other was thinking.

Kate and I clambered up from our cross-leggedness and went out the beachside door in front of Uncle Charlie. Mom, Dad, Aunt Ruth and two trays with cold drinks and a big bowl of finger-staining raspberries and strawberries greeted us.

"So, what's the progress report?" Dad cocked an eyebrow as he handed Kate the bowl. Not one to let a good idea pass her by, Kate told everyone about pirates along the shore. I could tell by Dad's grin that he was going to let his imagination run, "You don't s'pose they buried stuff under the boathouse do you?"

I laughed so hard, the way Kate's tongue shot out and her eyes went like saucers! Her red fingers smacked her cheeks and it was all Mom could do to stop her from charging back into the boathouse to get to pirate treasure. If only someone had brought the camera down from the house — what a picture of Kate!

The prospect of finding something other than beach rocks underneath the rotten boards was just too much of a pull for we girls to be sociable much longer. "Please, Uncle Charlie, let's go back and work some more. Please!"

As he got out of his deck chair, Dad said, "It's all right, Charlie, I'll go in with them for a while. C'mon girls, let's go pull a few boards." With that, Kate and I led the way back into the wobbling puddles of sunshine, especially back to our slippery plank, which just had to be the one covering the long-hidden treasure.

"Kate, slow down, watch your feet, don't slip," echoed off the narrow walls as Dad caught up to and steadied my little sister, "and don't get your hopes up, there are lots of places along this shore where pirates might have landed."

None of Dad's words that day really did much to dampen our eagerness to lever ourselves closer to something other than sea-smoothed rocks. For a few minutes, no one said anything as our thoughts ran to pirate days. "Dad, do you think pirates fell in love with girls who lived on the shore?" I asked, being rather more of a romantic than my younger sister, even then.

"Oh, I daresay there was many a pirate conspiring in those days. I would have taken a fancy to your mother were I a pirate at the time," he grinned and winked at me.

"Yuuuckeee, why do you think of that instead of treasure, Chris?" a determined Kate stopped to add. "Treasure's the thing."

With an I-know-more-than-she-does glance at Dad, I bent over my board, "You go for your treasure and I'll go for mine, Kate. That's OK."

The twisted and stubborn nail that Uncle Charlie had loosened earlier finally let its board break away as Kate gave one more tug. If I thought her tongue couldn't come out of her mouth any further or her eyes gone any bigger than they did at snack time, I'd have been dead wrong. She all but fell face-first into the space beneath the board!

As Dad and I leaned her way, we saw something sticking up from the rocks under the shed. "No way!" I yelped, as Kate's curls bounced back and forth behind Dad's cautious hand.

"Well girls, I guess we've found something but, please Kate, let me get it. That looks like metal and it might well be sharp. I don't want anyone getting cut here. Your Aunt Ruth would not be amused," Dad said, as he gently but firmly moved Kate's hands further away from the grimy shape near the old nail.

I don't really remember what I was thinking at that moment but I do know that both of us were sitting pretty still with our hearts in our mouths (as Mom would say) while Dad used the small pry-bar to uncover the greenish slippery treasure. It was pretty small, so I silently decided it wasn't one of Kate's imagined treasured chests, but it was something, and it seemed to take ages for Dad to free it from the rocks and wet sand.

"Let's share this with the others," said Dad as he cradled the little box in one hand and helped us to our feet. Kate's glee echoed ahead of her as we hurried onto the dock to Mom, Aunt Ruth and Uncle Charlie.

As we all held our breath, spare napkins cleaned off the little metal box and Uncle Charlie's screwdriver gently prised open one rotting end. Dad's careful fingers reached inside and pulled out a tiny package. In the warm sun by the bay with our favourite people around us, Kate and I watched in amazed silence as, out of the wrapping, a tiny gold locket opened into our dad's hands to reveal a dried blue forget-me-not.

TINA MARDEL STEWART grew up in St. John's, Gander and Corner Brook, graduated from Memorial University, married, and moved some more. She has lived in the United States and on islands in the Caribbean, and has written about life with children and grandchildren. She now calls Kelligrews, Conception Bay South, home.

Pam Frampton is a columnist and the story editor at The Telegram. She has a BA (Honours) in English Literature from Memorial University and has worked as a journalist for 20 years. Originally from Trinity Bay, she lives in St. John's with her husband, videojournalist Glenn Payette, their two wonderful teenagers and their furry, four-legged son. An ardent fan of books and language, Pam was a founding member of The Telegram's literary prize committee and is its current chair.